THE ITALIAN PLAYBOY'S SECRET SON

THE ITALIAN PLAYBOY'S SECRET SON

BY

REBECCA WINTERS

MILLS & BOON®
Pure reading pleasure™

First published in Great Britain 2008
Large Print edition 2008
Harlequin Mills & Boon Limited,
Eton House, 18-24 Paradise Road,
Richmond, Surrey TW9 1SR

ISBN: 978 0 263 20079 9

Set in Times Roman 16½ on 19 pt.
16-0908-52590

Printed and bound in Great Britain
by Antony Rowe Ltd, Chippenham, Wiltshire

CHAPTER ONE

"Two more laps and it's yours, Cesar."

Nothing was ever "yours" until you crossed the finish line with the best time, but he didn't say that to his crew chief talking to him through the mic in his helmet.

"You're coming up on turn four. Watch out for Prinz. He's starting to make his run."

"I see him."

"Rykert has hit the cement wall. There's debris. Go inside."

Cesar made the correction. Coming out of the turn he saw what was left of Rykert's car. Smoke poured from it like a genie escaping a bottle. Then his heart failed him as part of Prinz's chassis flew at Cesar out of nowhere. Zero hope of escape. This was it.

"I'm a dead man."

No sooner did the words leave his mouth than

the impact of gut-crunching debris tossed him in an arc across the track. He experienced blinding flashes of light before being sucked into an acrid-smelling black vortex.

"Cesar?"

He felt hands on his shoulders, shaking him gently.

"Cesar?"

Cesar de Falcon, known as Cesar Villon in the Formula 1 racing world, awakened gasping for breath. His torso was vibrating like a jackhammer. He saw his doctor leaning over him with a concerned look in his eyes.

"You're all right, Cesar. Your nightmares about the crash have begun. Do you remember any of them?"

"No." Everything from after a tire change at his last pit stop until he awoke in a hospital in Sao Paulo was a complete blank to him. He lifted an arm to wipe the perspiration off his forehead. His body was lying in a pool of sweat.

"I'll see you're bathed and changed immediately."

While Cesar waited for his heart rate to slow

down, two of the nursing staff came in to clean him up and change his bed. Then his doctor was back.

"They left your breakfast, but I see you haven't touched it yet."

Still shuddering from the nightmare of a crash he couldn't remember, the last thing he wanted was food. "Feed it to some poor devil who gives a damn."

What he needed was a pill to keep him awake so he wouldn't have to experience another night of nameless terror like last night. But being awake proved to be equally horrendous.

He lay on his back, unable to move his legs.

Dead from the waist down.

Six years before his heart had also died. His demise was now complete.

"Your physical therapy *must* begin today."

One bronzed arm covered his eyes. "Why?"

"Surely I shouldn't have to point out that you need to keep up your strength in order to get through it." The doctor spoke as if Cesar hadn't said anything. "Putting it off any longer won't help you walk again," he said as he took Cesar's vital signs.

Cesar grabbed the doctor's hand to prevent him

from doing anything more. "It isn't going to happen. Save your speech for someone who's gullible enough to believe it. Don't you understand? Look at me!" The cords stood out in his neck. "I've lost my body and my mind."

"You're only feeling that way because your nightmare is still upon you. But believe me—you're alive and well in every other way. I've told you repeatedly it's too soon to tell if there's permanent damage to your spine. After that crash on the track, it's a miracle you're in such good sha—"

"Get out, *dottore!*"

The rage in his voice sent a shudder through Sarah Priestley's body. She'd been standing outside the hospital room door. The doctor had left it open, making it possible for her to see and hear Cesar for herself so she'd know what she was up against.

Though she didn't speak or understand Italian, his violent response revealed the depth of his despair. Sarah cringed, unable to imagine what life must be like for him now.

As the doctor came out of the room, he took her aside. "Cesar had a very bad night. I'm positive he was dreaming about the crash, but he couldn't recall it when he woke up. It's his mind I'm worried about. He needs to remember in order to help the healing process. Everything else is good. His body is strong and healthy, which is vitally important in his case.

"Unfortunately he won't stay that way long if he refuses to eat or get started on crucial therapy. He's like a wounded animal that won't let anyone come near."

"Then he's got to be lured out of that dark place where he's living," she whispered, sick at heart for him. Until now he'd walked away from his other track accidents without severe injury.

Sarah had always feared there would come a time when the law of averages caught up to him. Now that day was here…

The doctor nodded for her to go in, but his expression said that she entered at her own risk.

Risk was right!

But Sarah had to do this. Yesterday she'd flown from San Francisco to Rome with her son, Johnny. A taxi had taken them to their hotel. From there they'd come straight to the hospital.

After being denied information or access to

Cesar since he'd declared himself strictly off-limits, she'd made an appointment to talk to the doctor. But until he'd seen Johnny with his own eyes, he'd refused to discuss the case with her. At that point he was forced to concede that Sarah and Cesar had a history together and agreed to tell her what he knew.

To her dismay she learned Cesar had refused all visitors, including his parents and brother who were starting to panic. If there was an important woman in his life at the moment, the doctor had no knowledge of her. Cesar had demanded to be left alone.

With the exception of his private personal hospital staff brought in to take care of the absolute basics, he'd been given his wish. Since being flown to Italy after the ghastly crash on the racetrack in Brazil a week ago, Cesar had gone downhill steadily. No one could get through to him.

"Is it true then he's suicidal?" she'd asked the doctor yesterday, dreading the answer. "I heard it on television, but I didn't believe it. That doesn't sound like Cesar. He's a fighter."

The doctor frowned. "He's in a severe depression. Frankly I'm worried he's reaching that stage."

She shuddered. "Tell me about his injury."

"The chain of nerve cells that runs from the brain through the spinal cord out to the muscle is called the motor pathway. Normal muscle function requires intact connections all along that pathway. Cesar's has been damaged in one area, enough to have reduced the brain's ability to control the muscle movements in his legs.

"After studying all the X-rays, I have reason to believe it's only badly bruised. In time there could be nerve regrowth. Therefore he needs to be undergoing physical therapy to retrain his limbs. It will maintain and build any strength and control that remain in the affected muscles."

"Then it's not impossible that he'll get feeling back!"

"No."

That was all she needed to hear. "Does he know he has everything to live for?"

The doctor nodded. "But his mind—despairing and traumatized by the nightmares—is keeping him from believing it."

"How soon can I see him, Doctor?"

He eyed her speculatively. "Your visit could be the kind of shock therapy Cesar needs to provoke a reaction from him. I'll arrange it for tomorrow morning."

"Thank you." It was worth anything if she could pull him out of the black sinkhole burying him alive.

"I'm counting on you, Signorina Priestley," he murmured in a grave tone.

Little did the doctor know she was counting on *Johnny…*

If Sarah hadn't witnessed for herself Cesar's precarious mental state in front of the doctor just now, she might not have found the courage to follow through with her plan. But the situation called for drastic measures.

One of the nurses named Anna was keeping her son company at the nursing station down the hall. She spoke enough English to communicate with him. When it was time, Sarah would get him and bring him to the hospital room. Of course that depended on Cesar…

After taking a fortifying breath, she stepped over the threshold into his territory.

A thin sheet covered the lower half of his body where he lay flat in the bed. Sarah could hardly tell he'd been in a crash, one that neither he nor the two other drivers could have prevented. It had sent all of them to the hospital. Cesar had been the most seriously injured.

Her heart quaked. *Cesar—my love—*

His millions of adoring fans located throughout the world would be horrified to see the great Cesar Villon, five time world champion of the Formula 1 Grand Prix, lying helpless in a hospital bed, unable to move his legs. The cruel media had already predicted he was crippled for life.

He was part Italian through his mother's titled Varano family, and part Monegasque through his titled father, the Duc de Falcon of Monaco. Between a week's growth of black beard and his black curly hair more unruly than usual, the thirty-three-year-old race car driver was the epitome of the ultimate, dashing, aristocrat bachelor.

With his eyes closed, the black lashes against his gorgeous olive skin accentuated the bruised hollows beneath, the only surface evidence of the crash's impact. It was a miracle he'd survived something that had demolished the fabulous race car his engineering brother Luc de Falcon had designed several years ago.

Called the Faucon, the French name for falcon,

toy manufacturers had made a facsimile of it. Her son had a collection of miniature Formula 1 race cars, but he prized his daddy's Faucon. In fact he was the keeper of the scrapbook they'd kept about his famous father. He pored over it every night before saying his prayers.

When she was a few feet from the left side of Cesar's bed, she finally found the courage to speak. "H-hello, Cesar." Her voice faltered.

His eyes flew open.

The last time she'd seen him in person, they'd been a beautiful, translucent gray burning with desire for her. These eyes were the color of a dark funnel cloud that had touched ground, destroying everything in its path.

Her mouth went dry. She couldn't swallow. "I-it's good to see you again after so long," she stammered.

At thirty-three, he was more attractive than ever. But the low, menacing curse that escaped his bloodless lips was evidence that Sarah was the last person Cesar had expected to see walk into his room.

She supposed it was at least something that he still recognized her.

The last time they'd been together she'd been twenty, and proud of the fact that she'd never cut the hair that had hung down her back to her waist.

Six years later it was now styled in a jaw-length feather cut, bringing out the oval of her face, and dark fringed eyes.

Time had added curves to her slim, five-foot-seven body. His narrowed gaze took in all of her. Heat filled her cheeks to realize he knew every centimeter of what lay beneath the soft crepe dress in periwinkle covering her figure. If anything, he looked repulsed by her.

This was so much worse than she'd imagined, and Sarah had thought she'd imagined the worst—

"You once asked me to join you in Italy." She took a fortifying breath. "Until now there was a good reason why I didn't."

"Your timing's off," sounded the frigid voice before he closed his eyes against her.

Clearly this conversation was over as far as he was concerned.

Though she was terrified of the change in him, she held her ground. "I disagree. The next racing season doesn't start until March. That gives you seven months to recover from this temporary setback. There couldn't be a better time for my visit."

"Go away, Sarah." She could feel his white-hot rage boiling beneath the surface.

"I'm glad you still remember my name."

Another Italian curse pierced the air. Anyone else would have flown from the room by now, but she was on a desperate mission.

"Surely you're not taking back the invitation you once extended me."

"Get the hell out of here—"

All pretense of civility had fled.

While his brutal demand bounced off the walls of the room, his dark head had turned away from the entrance. He'd closed his eyes, undoubtedly believing he'd scared her off for good.

"I don't pity you, you know," she persevered. "The doctor told me you're going to walk again. In truth, I came for an entirely different reason."

Any sensible person would have stayed away, but she wasn't just any person, sensible or not. She'd given birth to Cesar's son. Now was the moment for them to meet.

Heaven help me, her heart cried as she stood there shaking from the inside out.

"Maybe you don't remember what you said to me the morning after we made love, but I do. You said, Sarah? With two more races coming up and the extra practice time I need to put in testing out a new tire, you and I won't be able to be together again like this for a couple of months.

"'When I'm free, I'll send for you to join me for two weeks in Positano like we talked about. After that I'll have to get ready for a race coming up in France, and after that Spain.'"

She shifted her weight nervously. "I would have come for those two weeks, but by the time you phoned me to make final plans, I had just learned some news that would alter both our lives forever."

Another unintelligible epithet escaped his lips.

This was it.

"I—I discovered I was…pregnant."

This brought his head around. His eyes opened to slits. "Pregnant with whose child?" he lashed out, his words dripping acid.

It was hard to breathe. "Yours."

He swore savagely. "Tell me another story. I took precautions."

"I know, but my obstetrician told me no protection is a hundred percent. In case you wanted proof, I brought the results of his DNA with me."

"His?"

"You and I have a little boy, Cesar. He looks so much like you, the nursing staff can't get over it."

In that instant she heard his breath catch in shock.

"*I* have a *son?*"

Despite his fragile state and his anger toward her, she'd heard unmistakable joy in his voice just now. He couldn't disguise it. That was all she needed to know to carry out the rest of her plan.

"Yes. Since his birth, it's been just the two of us. He's at the nursing station waiting impatiently to meet his famous father."

His face paled. "If this is some kind of joke—"

"It isn't! I swear before God. Give me a moment and I'll be right back with him."

When Cesar didn't tell her no, she hurried out of the room. Johnny saw her and came running toward her. "Hi, honey." She swept him into her arms, wanting to cry out in pain for Cesar who'd been through too much. But she couldn't break down in front of Johnny.

"Did you talk to daddy?" he wanted to know immediately.

"Yes."

"Does he want to see me?"

She hugged him tighter. Cesar's cry of amazement still rang in her ears. He wanted to see Johnny all right. "Of course he does!"

"Is he very sick?"

"No. With a lot of exercise he's going to be fine." *He had to be.*

Johnny seemed satisfied with her answer.

The first time he was old enough to ask about his daddy, she'd explained that his father didn't know about Johnny because he'd gone away long before he was born.

As time wore on and he grew more curious, she told him about Cesar and showed him pictures. She assured him that when the time was right, she would take him to meet his busy father. Finally her son was going to get his wish.

She looked down at Johnny, hoping against hope this first meeting wouldn't end in disaster. Two precious lives were at stake here. Both were so vulnerable. If anything went wrong now…

With her heart racing like the engine of Cesar's Formula 1 car, she took hold of

Johnny's hand and they started down the hall toward his hospital room.

Maybe Cesar was in the middle of a dream…

He *had* to be dreaming. His hands balled into fists.

Long ago he'd dispatched memories of Sarah Priestley to the ends of the universe. In the intervening years he hadn't known where she'd gone, or what had happened to her. She'd killed all his feelings for her.

What he'd experienced just now had to be her shadow left over from his nightmare.

You and I have a little boy.

No…

Impossible…

Once upon a time when he'd been wildly in love with her, he'd wondered what it would be like to see her pregnant and watch her beautiful body undergo the changes. But before his imaginings had had the barest hope of becoming a reality, she'd dealt him the death blow.

Right now he needed something strong to blot her out permanently from his subconscious. Panicked, he reached for the button to call the nurse. In the process of doing so he heard a slightly husky feminine voice say, "Honey? This is your daddy."

With those words Cesar's head snapped around. He opened his eyes. There she was again, this time accompanied by a child.

A boy.

A Falcon, as he lived and breathed.

Solemn gray-blue eyes stared at Cesar for the longest time. "I didn't know you had a beard, Daddy. You look different."

Oh, Johnny—

"My papa Priestley says hair makes your skin itch."

Sarah saw the stunned expression on Cesar's face. It prompted her to say, "The doctors have kept your daddy so busy trying to help him get better, he hasn't had time to shave yet. Maybe that's why he's a little grumpy. Kind of reminds me of you when you haven't had enough sleep."

The tension in the room was so thick, she almost lost courage to finish the long overdue introduction. Never would she have imagined it happening under these emotionally perilous circumstances.

"Cesar? I'd like you to meet your son. His birth certificate lists his name as Jean-Cesar Priestley de Falcon, named after you and your father Jean-Louis. Around our house he's known as Johnny Priestley. Your Italian mother will probably call him Giovanni.

"We flew all this way to tell you we're sorry you were hurt in that accident, but we know that pretty soon you're going to be all better."

"Yup," Johnny said. His troubled eyes remained fastened on his father. "We saw you crash on TV. Somebody said you died—" his voice trembled "—but Mommy said you didn't. She promised I could come to see you."

Cesar sat up in the bed abruptly. His action drew her attention to his hard-muscled body covered by the flimsy hospital gown. She noted with satisfaction there was nothing wrong with his reflexes above the waist. He had the most stringent workout ethic known in the racing world. A hundred sit-ups a session was nothing for him.

Though she'd tried to prepare him, Sarah could tell he was so astonished, he still couldn't speak.

"Do your legs hurt?" The fearful question asked in total innocence couldn't have helped but move Cesar who was examining his son in utter disbelief.

Like a man with shell shock he gave a barely perceptible negative shake of his head.

"That's good. Can't you talk?" Johnny asked in alarm.

Sarah saw incredulity in Cesar's eyes before they softened and he said, "Come closer," in a husky voice.

She held her breath as Johnny slowly let go of her hand and walked to the edge of the bed. In a deft masculine movement, Cesar reached for him with those strong, bronzed arms and lifted him onto his lap.

While they studied each other, no conversation passed between them. Both were too fascinated to be aware of her.

Sarah had lavender-gray eyes. They produced the flecks of blue in the gray eyes she and Cesar had bequeathed to Johnny. Her sable hair mixed with Cesar's black hair combined to give their curly headed boy his unique dark hair color.

The rest of him was Cesar's contribution. Besides his olive skin, Johnny possessed enough of the de Falcon and Varano genes in his aquiline features to scream paternity simply by looking at him. He was on the taller side for his age. Talk about Cesar's little lookalike—

"Was that crash scary?" Johnny sounded like he was going to cry, but he was manfully holding back the tears.

She heard Cesar clear his throat. "It happened too fast for me to be scared," he explained in the heavily accented voice that still haunted Sarah's dreams.

"Last week I was riding my bike and crashed into a fire hydrant."

"Did it hurt?" Cesar asked.

"Yes. See my scab?" He raised his pant leg to his knee for his father to inspect. "Mommy put a bandage on it, but it came off."

"That was a pretty big fall."

Johnny nodded. "I cried. Carson told me I was a crybaby."

"Is Carson your friend?"

"Yes."

"Sometimes you can't help it."

"I bet *you* didn't cry."

There were other ways of crying, but Johnny

was too young to realize his father was hurting inside. Anxious to change the subject Sarah said, "Do you know what, honey? The doctor told us we could only stay a few minutes. We need to let daddy rest now. He's not used to visitors."

"But, Mom—"

"Johnny's my son, not a visitor," Cesar interjected in that authoritative tone instinctive to him. His acknowledgment of ownership had the undeniable ring of possession. The reaction was so much more than Sarah could have hoped for.

A suntanned hand lifted to tousle the smaller head of dark curls in a fatherly gesture. Johnny was the kind of boy any father would kill to claim for his own. "I'm not in the least tired."

"See, Mommy? Daddy wants us to stay."

Her plan to shock Cesar out of his damaging psychological torpor had succeeded. But this was only the first step. Once she was alone with Cesar, he would take out his fury on her. He had every right.

She didn't expect him to forgive her for keeping their son a secret all these years. Never that. However she was confidant he wouldn't exact his revenge in front of Johnny who'd already seduced his father by simply being the adorable, handsome son of his loins.

Her gaze flicked to Cesar. "If you're really not too tired, do you mind if I eat some of your breakfast? We left the hotel early, and I'm afraid I'm hungry." In actuality she felt faint and reached for an orange, needing the sugar. While she started to peel it, her fingers trembled.

"I'm hungry, too!" Johnny chimed in. "We both had tummy aches this morning, Daddy."

"Is that so," he muttered, but Sarah heard him.

"Yes. I guess your tummy hurts, too," Johnny said, eyeing the full tray.

Cesar had just found out that little boys have big eyes as well as ears.

Sarah extended the roll plate. Johnny took two of them and bit into one. "Mmm. This is good. Here, Daddy."

She was secretly delighted to see that Cesar had little choice but to accept the other roll and take a bite.

"I don't like hospitals," Johnny declared. "Do you?"

"No." The one syllable answer told its own story.

"Do you have to stay in here a long time?"

While she held her breath waiting for the answer she heard Cesar say, "As a matter of fact I'm planning to go home before the day is out."

After Cesar's outburst with the doctor, she could believe it. Knowing how much he loved his freedom, he would feel like a caged animal in here. If she'd arrived a day later it would have been much more difficult to track him down…

"Do you want to come to our house?" came the timid question.

She could hear Cesar's mind working. "In Carmel?"

"Nana and Papa live there. Mommy and I live in Watsonville. In a *town house*."

Close enough to be near the grandparents, far enough away from the racing world for no one to ever make the connection between Johnny and his legendary father.

Avoiding Cesar's probing gaze she said, "Here's some grape juice for you, honey."

"Thanks." He drank several swallows. "Do you want some, Daddy?" His purple moustache was so cute.

"I think I do."

The sight of Johnny seated on Cesar's lap with

the two of them drinking from the same glass melted Sarah's heart.

Would knowing he had a son force him to realize he had someone else to live for now? Someone who loved him without qualification? The doctor had said Cesar was fast losing the will to live.

Please, God, let Johnny be the inspiration Cesar needed to dig deep inside himself and fight his way back to a quality life, whatever that might be.

While Sarah finished eating the orange slices, Johnny started asking Cesar questions about the buttons on the remote. Soon he'd pressed all of them. He loved the one that raised the head of the bed so his father could rest against it. Cesar didn't seem to mind.

Suddenly an older nurse appeared in the room. Her eyes widened to see how totally things had changed since Johnny's arrival. Cesar said something unintelligible to her. She nodded as if she were in a daze, then left in a hurry.

"How come you talk different?"

"Because people here speak Italian," she answered. "Your father also speaks French and Spanish, Johnny."

He looked over at her. “We speak American.”

“No, honey. We speak English.”

Johnny pondered everything and then turned to his father. “What did you say to that lady?” Sarah wanted the answer to that question, too.

“I told her to bring me a razor.”

Johnny’s eyes lit up. “Can I watch you shave?”

“You’d like that?” Cesar sounded amused.

“Yes!”

Sarah made a snap decision. “Since shaving is a guy thing, I’ll slip out to the rest room down the hall to wash my hands, then I’ll be right back. Is that okay with you, honey?”

“Yes.”

If she’d left him with anyone else, Johnny would have run after her. Instead she’d gotten an unworried response because he was with his remarkable father at last. For the moment all was right with his world.

As she was leaving the room, she heard him tell Cesar, “Mommy was going to take me to see you race, but you crashed in that other race first.”

Johnny had held her to the promise she’d made him to get all three of them together at the U.S. Monterey Grand Prix taking place next month.

He'd been living for it. But the accident in Brazil had changed the timing.

Her heart thumping painfully in her breast, she hurried down the hall to the ladies' room. Thankfully no one else was inside the lounge part. She only made it as far as the upholstered banquette before sinking down on it.

It was one thing to suffer guilt over having kept the knowledge of their son from Cesar all these years. The burden had been unbearable, but to see the two of them together at last—to see and feel how much he wanted Johnny and how much Johnny wanted him, deepened her anguish to the point where she felt she could die of remorse.

Sarah hugged her arms to her body, rocking back and forth. What had she done?

"If I were in your place, I would never be able to forgive me, either, Cesar. I don't deserve to live, but that's my punishment." In torment she buried her face in her hands and sobbed.

When the tears finally stopped flowing she lifted her head. On trembling legs she got up to rinse her face and try to repair the damage from her breakdown.

Once she'd refreshed her lipstick, she felt more

in possession of herself and left the lounge. The doctor was waiting for her at the nursing station with a pleased expression on his face.

"Your boy is responsible for a minor miracle happening this morning, Signorina Priestley."

"I know." She wiped her eyes, still shaken by the encounter with Cesar after all this time. If the doctor only knew the worst was yet to come.

"You didn't arrive here any too soon. Cesar plans to leave the hospital today."

"I heard him say as much to Johnny."

"You must convince him he *has* to get started on a regimen of physical therapy. At this juncture every minute he works on his recovery is vital."

"I realize that. Unfortunately I have no influence over him, but it's possible Johnny's existence will provide the needed incentive."

"It has already. Wanting to shave is an indication he's coming back to life."

"You're right. Thank you for everything you've done for him."

"He's an icon in my country. What a tragedy if he lets this experience defeat him."

"Not if Johnny and I can help it." She shook his hand before heading for Cesar's room.

Almost at the door she met the nurse coming out with the empty food tray. Johnny didn't like eggs, so Cesar must have eaten them. Even if he'd only done that to humor his son, it was better than nothing.

When Sarah walked inside, the first thing she saw was a clean shaven Cesar talking on the phone in rapid-fire Italian from his bed. His transformation back to the physically arresting man she remembered made her breath catch.

She felt his searing glance on her features. Anyone could tell she'd been crying, but it would mean less than nothing to him. Why should it?

He was sitting in an upright position against the mattress. Even without the use of his legs, he had a virile presence that turned her limbs to water.

Johnny stood on a chair pulled up next to him. When he saw her he cried, "Look, Mommy—" He was playing with the electric razor lying among the loose hair that had fallen on the table and settled across Cesar's lap.

A boy toy, one he'd never seen around their town house.

Without saying anything, she took it from him and rolled the table away to clean everything up.

In the process she noticed a few gray hairs among the black, evidence that Cesar was six years older than the last time they'd been together. She was six years older, too, and had the stretch marks to prove it.

But the years had only added a few character lines to his face, enhancing the dark, handsome looks every female fan went crazy over. Sometimes she couldn't believe he'd desired her enough to make love to her all night long. Not until she looked at Johnny, who would be a heartbreaker like his father when he was all grown up.

"Johnny?" his father asked the second he'd ended his cell phone call. The name sounded so different when he said it in his heavy Italian accent. "I need to talk to your mother in private. You met Anna a little while ago. She's going to come and take you down to the hospital restaurant for a treat. You can have anything you want. How does that sound?"

"Will it take a long time for you to talk to Mommy?"

Cesar's eyes swerved to Sarah's with piercing intensity. They seemed to say that the answer depended entirely on her. "Not too long."

"Promise?"

"Promise."

"Okay."

With perfect timing, the attractive young nurse poked her head in the door. "*Ciao,* Johnny. Come with me. We will get a soda. Is that good?"

He nodded and jumped down from the chair.

Sarah gave him a little hug and walked him to the door. "See you in a few minutes, honey."

The nurse smiled at Sarah, sending her a private message that she'd keep him occupied as long as possible. "I will take good care of him."

Johnny looked up at the other woman. "You don't have to take good care of me. I can do it myself."

Anna laughed. "You sound like your papa. You look like him, too!"

When they left, Sarah shut the door. A shiver swept through her body. For the moment she was enclosed in the room with a man whose enmity reached out to her like a living thing.

CHAPTER TWO

"I MUST confess that if I'd put in an order for the perfect son, I couldn't have imagined any child as marvelous in every way as Johnny," he began in a deceptively silken voice. "But for the crash, it begs the question whether I would ever have known him otherwise..."

"Cesar—" She turned to him. Sarah had thought she could handle this, but now she wasn't so sure. "I—I planned for you to meet him when you came to Calif—"

"*Basta—*" He cut her off abruptly. "The only thing I care to discuss with you is our son's future. You've had everything your own way all this time. He's bonded to you. I could take him away from you legally. In case it has slipped your mind, I have more financial resources than your father ever dreamed of having. But it would destroy Johnny and he would hate me for eternity. And I want equal rights over my child.

"For his sake the only solution is for us to marry."

Marry?

"No, Cesar—"

"No?" he inquired in a lethal tone.

She shuddered. "I mean, let's not talk about that right now. I—I know you despise me and you have every right. As for your family, they would never approve. The important thing here is—"

"For me to get well?" He snarled the question. "No doubt that's the fairy tale you've been reading to him since the accident last week, but it's never going to happen. By bringing an innocent child to my bedside and telling him I'm his father, you've put something into motion no one can undo now."

"I know that. Please listen to me—" she cried, trembling uncontrollably. His words had filled her with new fear, but Cesar was beyond noticing her reaction, or if he did, he didn't care.

"He's seen me in the flesh. He knows beyond any doubt I exist. To *not* make him an official Falcon, my legitimate heir, would be a mortal sin I have no wish to carry to the grave. I leave the heinous sin of omission to weigh on your seductive shoulders, *bellissima.*"

"It *does* weigh, Cesar. More heavily than you can imagine. But you never wa—"

"Never wanted marriage before?" he lashed out. "Is that what you were going to say?" A red flush had broken out beneath the skin on his cheeks. "The man you thought you once knew doesn't exist. That man could plant his seed in you and grow a *son!* That man could walk!"

His dark, frosty eyes glittered with rage. "The person you see before you would have to slither off this bed using his arms in order to drag his useless appendages close enough to reach you. Even then he would have to swipe at your legs to bring you down to his level so he could wrap his hands around the slender column of your beautiful white neck and strangle you for what you've done."

Her horrified gasp brought a cruel smile to his lips. "But I can think of a much better way to wring down retribution on your head. Johnny tells me there's a *nice guy* named Mick who comes to the town house *all* the time."

Knowing the erroneous construction Cesar had

already put on that information, Sarah's hands curled around the nearest chair back for support.

"Mick sells 'surance," Cesar imitated their son to perfection. "He comes to dinner a lot and he brings me toys. After I go to bed he stays and watches movies with her."

"Mick's a friend, Cesar. Nothing more," she said quietly. "You know I had never been intimate with a man before you, and there's been no one else since." Sarah couldn't. There was no man to equal him.

A frightening curse escaped his throat. "And this is supposed to absolve you of any wrongdoing?"

"No— I'm only trying to explain about Mick because Johnny isn't old enough to understand yet."

"In that case neither you nor Mick should be bothered by any headlines the tabloids will print about our soon-to-be union. 'Nun marries eunuch after nonimmaculate conception six years earlier.'"

"*Cesar—*" His spirit was so black, she didn't know how to reach him.

"That's how the fairy tale reads, *cara mia.* Lest you've forgotten, let me refresh your memory.

"Once upon a time an enticing red-hot commoner with amethysts for eyes and dark flowing tresses, made incredible, passionate love with her words and her body all night long to a fool of a race car driver who happened to be the second born son of a duc.

"Alas, a curse was put upon them for indulging in such rapture. After she awoke from giving birth, she was no longer possessed by the cravings of the flesh and hid their son away. This was all accomplished unbeknownst to the second born son of the duc who awoke from his fiery crash to discover he was no longer a man."

"Stop it, Cesar!"

His menacing grin crucified her.

"Stop what? The truth? Something you never had the remotest possibility of telling until the pileup?" he ground out in a murderous tone. "You haven't heard the rest of this tale.

"The son grew up wondering if he had a father. 'Of course you have one,' his mother said. 'He's the one you can see on TV. They're pulling him out of that heap of rubble, which used to be three race cars, and they're taking him away in an ambulance. How would you like to go to the hospital and get a good look at what's left of him?'

"'In case his injuries are life-threatening, we wouldn't want him to die before you have a chance to call him Daddy at least one time, would we? I couldn't possibly live with that on my conscience.'

"'What's a conscience, Mommy?'"

Cesar leaned forward on his fist, ready to lunge at her. "I'd like the answer to that same question," he snarled. The tendons stood out in his bronzed neck. "Where was it when you first had an inkling you were pregnant? Did you ever once give it the slightest thought that I had the right to be *told?*"

Feeling faint she cried, "Do you think I haven't suffered every minute of every day and night for holding this back from you? But you are the Duc de Falcon's son, the world's greatest Formula 1 race car champion who'd had his career planned out for years before we met. A career that allowed no impediments to interfere. No wife, no children. *Niente*—you said. That meant nothing and no one!

"I was seventeen when I first heard that come

from your very lips. It was the same litany you repeated every time we saw each other including the night you took me to bed." She swallowed hard. "Those same words came out of your mouth as you slid out of our bed before leaving for your next race in France."

He looked as if despite his injuries he might well leap off the bed to shake her or worse. "Knowing I used protection with you, do you honestly think I would have blamed you if you'd told me we were expecting? One little phone call, Sarah. Just one. All I needed to hear were two words. 'I'm pregnant.'"

She shook her head while hot tears trickled down her cheeks. "At twenty years of age I was convinced those two little words would have brought embarrassment to your family and changed everything for you.

"I didn't want you to think I was one of those women who was out for anything I could get from you. And you'd convinced me that without total focus, your world standing as a champion would have been jeopardized."

A terrible sound emerged from his throat, frightening her. "Compared to our child being born, my career wins over the past five years mean *nothing* to me. How could you have professed to know me so well, yet not understand the most basic, elemental needs of my makeup?"

She groaned in pain. "I thought I did, but you're right, Cesar. At twenty years of age I had a fatal flaw that prevented me from taking my parents' advice and coming to you. I should have. I'll regret it for the rest of my life, but at the time I didn't even tell them the truth until I started to show.

"Mom and Dad gave me more than one lecture, so please don't blame them. To quote Daddy he said, 'Cesar shares equal responsibility in this. Anytime you sleep with someone, you take the risk of getting pregnant. Cesar knows that. He may be the greatest Formula 1 racer in recent history, but that doesn't absolve him of anything!'"

"Your father was right!" Cesar ground out.

"I know that now, but six years ago you had a race coming up in another month. I was terrified what the news might do to you, so I promised Daddy I would tell you when the time was right.

"He said, 'Cesar will always be preparing for another race. *Now* would be the time to tell him a new career has opened up, one fashioned expressly *by* him, *for* him! Your child will need him.'"

A terrible sound came from his throat. "And still you didn't come forward."

"I wish I could make you understand," she cried. "You'd been enjoying unprecedented success on the circuit. I—I didn't see how you could straddle fatherhood and racing without it affecting your career in precarious ways. I didn't want to be the reason your dreams were dashed, not after the way you'd talked so passionately about your plans.

"I—I couldn't do that to you or our baby who would be the real victim. Our child would suffer from only seeing you once in a while—that is if you wanted to be a father to it."

"*If* I wanted?" he raged, shaking his dark head.

Tears streamed down her face. "I was wrong, Cesar. Totally and completely wrong. My parents told me I'd live to regret it, but in the beginning I held back because I believed it was the right thing for both you and Johnny.

"In order not to cause you any embarrassment, I stayed away from anything to do with the racing world. No one knew about my past association with you.

"I thought maybe you'd come to my parents' home the next time you were in the States, but you never did. I took that as proof you never had the depth of feeling for me that I had for you."

"The way we left it, you were supposed to phone *me,* remember?" His voice sounded like thunder. "After waiting and waiting only to hear nothing from you after six months, why in the hell would I come around looking for you?"

"You wouldn't." Sarah couldn't prevent the sob that escaped. "There were so many times I started to phone you, but I lost my courage. By the time Johnny turned three and started asking questions about you, I determined to take him to Monaco so he could meet you. I had the tickets and was ready to fly over when I read in the tabloids about your involvement with a pregnant woman. It was another ugly scandal I refused to believe, but this time the woman turned out to be your brother Luc's fiancée, Cesar!"

His eyes were filled with pain and rage.

"I honestly didn't know what to do then. In case the baby turned out to be yours, I—I was afraid to fly there with Johnny and complicate matters. So I waited to hear. The time stretched. But there came a time when I realized I couldn't put Johnny off any longer and promised him we'd see you at your next race in Monterey.

"To my horror, you crashed on the track in Brazil before you could fly to California." Tears gushed from her eyes once more. "You'll never know the depth of my pain, Cesar." Without conscious thought she put a hand on his arm. "I'm devastated over what I've done to you."

His eyes bore holes into hers. "Devastated doesn't cover it." In a withering gesture he removed her hand. "I've missed out on Johnny's first five years of life." A bluish white ring had formed around his lips. "I want them back, but since that isn't possible, I'm demanding the rest of them. We're going to get married here at the hospital in a little while."

She wiped her cheeks with her palms. "No one can get married that fast."

He sucked in his breath. "*I* can. It's all been arranged."

As the man he was he could cut through his country's horrendous red tape, even produce a license on the spot.

"But you don't want to marry me," her voice trembled. "You never did or—"

"Or what?"

"N-nothing. It doesn't matter," she whispered.

He stared at her through shuttered lids. "I want my son. I'll do anything to have him, even if it means marrying his mother. After what you've denied me all this time, being condemned to bondage with a man who doesn't desire you—who couldn't do anything about it if he wanted to—might just be a suitable penance for you. Maybe there's some justice in this world after all."

She shook her head. "Take it out on me all you want, but don't let Johnny see how you feel when he's with us. The nurse will be bringing him back in a minute. He's so sweet and loving." Her voice broke.

"You mean the way you used to be?" he sneered. "It's strange. Once upon a time I thought I knew you."

"I guess we've both changed," she said in a raw tone. "You used to have a competitive spirit that nothing and no one could conquer."

"That was before I was put out of commission permanently."

"There's no definitive proof yet," she argued. "The doctor explained that yo—"

"I haven't finished," he said in a voice of ice. "There's only one reality. I'm paralyzed, so we'll start at that point with our son and go from there. I realize my being like this is repugnant to you, but *he* seems to be handling it well. With no expectation comes no future disappointment."

"You don't mean that!" Her heart couldn't take much more. "The doctor believes you'll walk again with hard work and therapy. So do I!"

He swore violently. "You'd better not have fed that lie to Johnny. Have I made myself clear?"

So crystal clear, he'd sent her into shock.

What she'd done to him was unconscionable. But for Cesar to have given up on himself gave proof of a dark side that terrified her. This couldn't be the same man she'd once known and would have given anything to marry.

She'd come to Rome nursing the faintest hope that when he saw Johnny, his anger toward her would soften. At least to the point where they could reason things out together for their son's welfare.

Instead she'd been met with an ultimatum that would bring her nothing but grief no matter what she did. The last thing in the world Cesar wanted was a wife, but he had to take her if he wanted his son. Ironically he was forced to offer marriage to the only person on earth he truly despised.

Sarah had no choice but to meet Cesar's demand. This situation wasn't about her. She knew that. It was about a father and son who needed each other in the most elemental of ways and deserved to know each other's love.

Johnny's happiness was on the line. There'd been too much hurt being deprived of his daddy all this time. To keep them apart now would create an untenable situation that would destroy three lives. She couldn't bear any more guilt on that score.

Sarah was desperate to make recompense, and vowed to dedicate the rest of her life to him and their son.

"Mommy? Daddy?"

Johnny came running into the room before Anna could stop him. Sarah thanked the other woman before shutting the door. Once the three of them were alone, Johnny ran over to the bed. "How come you talked so long?"

Cesar held back deliberately. He was waiting

to hear her say the words that would make her son's dreams come true. Johnny looked at her for the answer.

She moistened her lips nervously. "Your father and I had a lot to discuss, honey. H-he wants us to be a family."

"Like Carson's?"

"Yes." Carson had a mother and father who lived together. "Would you like that?"

He blinked before turning to his daddy once more. "You mean you're going to *live* with us?" The wonder in his voice brought tears to Sarah's eyes. She could only imagine what Cesar must be feeling right now.

"You and your mommy are going to live with *me*. In fact I insist on it."

"Hooray!"

Without conscious thought her gaze flew to Cesar whose eyes remained veiled in front of their son. Like black ice they hid his full fury. She'd caught some of it while they'd been alone. Whenever he got her on his own again, he would unleash a little more and a little more.

Her legs shook. The thought of living with him under these circumstances petrified her.

Not so Johnny who was gazing at his father with pure joy. "Where's your house?"

"You mean *our* house." Johnny nodded with happiness. "We have two houses."

"Two?" he cried in astonishment.

"That's right. One is in Monaco where my parents and brother live."

"Is that far away?"

"Pretty far. We'll go there soon and visit your de Falcon relatives."

"Mommy said I have a grandma and a grandpa, and an uncle Luc."

Cesar's eyes flashed in surprise. "That's right. He and your aunt Olivia have a little daughter named Marie-Claire. She's your cousin."

"Can I play with her sometime?"

"Of course. But for right now we're going to our other house. It's here in Italy in a town called Positano. It sits way up on a hillside overlooking the ocean."

"I *love* the ocean."

"Then it's settled."

Six years ago Cesar had asked Sarah to join him in Positano for a two-week vacation. That seemed a century ago.

Cesar leaned toward Johnny. “Have you ever flown in a helicopter?”

“No. Have you?”

“All the time.”

“Is it scary?”

“Were you scared on the plane?” Cesar countered with another question.

“Nope.”

“Then you don’t need to worry about flying to the villa with me.”

“What’s a villa?”

“That’s another name for a house.”

Johnny was ecstatic. “When can we leave?”

“Right after your mother and I get married.”

His eyes rounded. “But we’re in the hospital.”

“This hospital has a chapel downstairs on the second floor. Our family priest is coming to officiate. Tell you what. While your mother goes back to the hotel for your bags, you can help me get ready.”

“I *want* to help!”

Judging by the sudden telltale sheen filming Cesar’s eyes, their darling boy had already worked his way into his father’s heart.

"In that case, push this button and the nurse will come and organize us."

Johnny reached for it. "Okay. I did it!"

This was Sarah's cue to leave. She gave her son a kiss on the cheek. "I'll be back in a little while."

He nodded, but it was clear Johnny had much more exciting things on his mind. Getting a father had to be at the top of the list.

"Don't be long."

Cesar's warning almost made her stumble. As she was going out the door, two male nurses came into the room. With Cesar's fiery gaze on her retreating back, she was glad to be able to escape, if only to remove the tension for Johnny's sake.

By sending her to the hotel alone, it was clear he wasn't taking the chance that she would change her mind and disappear with their son. Surely he knew she would never do that, otherwise she wouldn't have dreamed of bringing Johnny to Italy in the first place.

She left the hospital and took a taxi to the Bernini Palace Hotel about a mile away. Her packing didn't take long. Not knowing how long they'd be in Italy, she hadn't brought many clothes for either of them. Certainly nothing appropriate to wear at her own wedding. Yet she didn't dare hold up Cesar's schedule by shopping for an outfit. To add more crimes to the unforgivable one didn't bear thinking about.

However she'd forgotten that August was the heavy month for tourists pouring into Rome. While she stood in line waiting to check out at the reception desk, she was tormented by her inability to help Cesar understand her frame of mind six years ago. The wall between them was too impenetrable.

Edward Priestley, Sarah's father, was the owner and CEO of the Quenchers soft drink company who'd built the Quenchers racetrack years earlier. It was near Carmel-By-The-Sea.

After the Formula 1 races, he always feted the top racers at their home in Carmel, a Spanish style hacienda overlooking the ocean. It was there that race aficionados gathered with the winners for celebrity photo shots and publicity.

Sarah had been going to the track with her parents and elder sister, Elaine, since she was a little girl. Having grown up with a father who lived and breathed racing, she knew his opinion about romantic entanglements with racers.

"Enjoy their talents, but keep your distance from them," he'd warned his girls. Her mother had said the same thing.

Elaine had listened, but the warning had gone right over the head of a young and foolish Sarah who hadn't taken their advice to heart until it was too late. At the age of seventeen she met Cesar Villon for the first time and developed a painful crush on the dashing twenty-four-year-old race car driver.

From that time on she followed his brilliant career and kept a scrapbook on him. Anything she could find in print about his life whether professional or personal. Whenever he was in the States for a race, he came to the Priestley home where she monopolized his time.

With each visit he sought her out and seemed to enjoy being with her more and more, often staying over at a hotel for several days. During those thrilling interludes they would take long walks along the surf together. Other times they went swimming and boating.

Whatever the activity, they never seemed to run out of things to talk about. She found herself pouring out her heart to him. He shared his dreams with her. Over time her feelings grew into a full-blown love that would never go away.

Cesar had dreams to win seven world championships. Seven was the magic number for him, a higher figure than anyone else in racing history. Then he would quit the circuit and run his business interests. At that point he would take on a wife and family who deserved his full attention.

Though she listened, she didn't really take it in. By the time she turned twenty, she didn't *want* to believe he would stay single that long. Her dream was to become his wife and bear his children as soon as possible.

So she continued to ignore what he kept telling her and played with fire until one night they made love. The experience changed her life forever.

But all he said was that she was the most wonderful girl he'd ever known, and he would make time for her in between racing schedules. Yet again he had reiterated that he had his career mapped out, and couldn't allow anything or anyone to interfere. Otherwise he might as well quit racing because family and Formula 1 didn't mix.

After their night of passion, she'd thought he would miss her so much that he would eventually change his mind and come after her. In her naivete she assumed he couldn't live without her, as she felt she couldn't live without him. She waited in vain for a declaration of love from him, let alone a proposal of marriage.

Two more races in two and a half months went by before he phoned to invite her to come to Italy for a two-week vacation. He'd prepaid her round-trip airfare.

Round-trip...

By then fate had thrown her a curve she hadn't anticipated. She was pregnant with his child, a child she adored from inception. It seemed part of her dream was now realized, but not the way she'd envisioned it. Cesar wasn't her husband nor likely to be in the near future.

If she told him the truth, she had no idea what he'd do. Some men would offer marriage because they were honorable and would want to give their child a name. As far as she was concerned, Cesar was honorable. But he came from a titled family in Monaco. Their prominence guaranteed they wouldn't be thrilled to learn a no account American girl was carrying one of the future heirs to the Falcon dynasty.

In all probability, Cesar would do what he could for their baby financially, but it would fall short of a full commitment. Any contact between them would be behind the scenes, when he was between races. Sarah didn't want her child's heart broken by a phantom father who showed up one day and went out of it the next.

What did she really know about Cesar? One thing was certain. Any feelings he had for her would die or turn to resentment because the pregnancy would have created complications that prevented him from achieving his goals. Too late she'd finally accepted that he'd really meant what he'd been saying all these years. He intended to stay single until he walked away from his career.

For the baby's sake, she knew what she had to do and turned down his invitation. She used the excuse that she couldn't leave college right then. In truth she had been close to graduating. Her biology classes went in a series and she couldn't afford to miss a course or she would have to repeat it the following year.

At first the line had gone quiet on his end. When he finally did speak, his disappointment sounded deep, if not profound, probably because he wasn't used to any woman turning him down. If he'd begged her, she would probably have lost her resolve to stay away, and would have flown there to tell him the news.

But unhappy as her words made him, he didn't try to persuade her otherwise. Instead he told her college was important and he understood. Therefore he would wait for a phone call from her when she could arrange to go on vacation with him.

He ended the conversation with, "I miss you, *bellissima.* You have no idea how much I long to have you here with me. Call me at the end of this semester and we'll work things out to be together."

Sick at heart, she realized a reunion with him would only last until the return date of the next round-trip ticket. Sarah had to face the bitter truth that he wasn't in love with her to the point that he couldn't live without her.

Now that he'd tossed the proverbial ball in her court, she could phone him back and tell him that he was going to be a father. But the news would change his world.

How could he possibly focus on his career with

a new baby needing his attention? Cesar required total freedom to get ready for each race. Such a distraction could severely affect his concentration. His career wasn't like other men's. Until she felt the right time presented itself, she would wait to tell him the truth.

But as it turned out, she never talked to him again.

After graduation she moved out of her parents' home in Carmel, and rented a small town house in nearby Watsonville where she found a job in an insurance firm. When she couldn't hide her pregnancy any longer, she told her parents who showed no surprise. They knew how much she loved Cesar.

Her mother's sad smile devastated Sarah because she'd urged her to stay away from Cesar when she could see what was happening to her daughter. "Besides having a powerful mistress you can't fight, he's an aristocrat whose family has already chosen someone suitable for him to marry. He'll only be trifling with you. If you're not careful, you're going to get hurt, sweetheart."

Sarah *had* gotten hurt. It was self-inflicted because she hadn't been able to stay away from Cesar. If she felt like she was a widow who'd never been a wife, she had no one to blame but herself.

But the hurt she'd inflicted on Cesar and her son by her silence went so much deeper there was no comparison. She couldn't give them back those years.

Sarah had done irreparable damage. How had she dared to play God with their lives?

With hindsight she could see and understand things she hadn't been capable of six years ago. Back then she'd been too young and immature. Too self-absorbed. She'd never given Cesar the chance to make a decision one way or the other.

She could thank providence it hadn't been too late for her to toss him an unexpected lifeline this morning in the form of his child. Perhaps the only one he would ever father. As for Johnny, he was safe at last in the arms of the daddy he'd always wanted.

But if Sarah had thought this reunion could wipe out those years of guilt and regret, she could think again.

No man could love the woman who'd done this to him. As for Johnny, one day when her son was older he would perceive what she'd done to be selfish and cruel. He would come to resent her, even dislike her for keeping him apart from his father all that time. The gulf between her and the two men she loved beyond all else would never be bridged.

Just deserts for the hell she could look forward to.

CHAPTER THREE

CESAR had asked one of the staff to run out and buy some things for him and Johnny. After being helped to get dressed in a new suit and tie, he picked up his phone again. He'd already made the necessary calls to get everything underway for the ceremony. Now he needed to alert his housekeeper to his plans.

While Johnny occupied himself with some paper and colored pens Anna had brought him, Cesar rang the villa.

"Pronto?"

"Bianca?"

"Cesario—" The sixty-five-year-old woman broke down and wept. "I've been to mass every day praying for you."

Touched by her motherly concern he said, "Someone upstairs heard you."

"You mean you can walk?" she blurted. "Your

parents haven't told me the news yet. Not even your brother, Luca."

"No, no, Bianca. That isn't going to happen. No one knows what I'm about to tell you except my doctor."

And Sarah of course.

His free hand crushed part of the bed sheet into a wad. When he'd invited her to come to Italy all those years ago, he'd believed she loved him with the kind of love a man would be lucky to know in one lifetime. She was his darling Sarah, a woman different from all the others. When she came, he would tell her… He had plans for them…

A curse flew from his lips. So much for that fiction. Now that he'd learned she'd kept his son from him all these years, he realized he hadn't known her at all. How could she of all people be capable of this kind of cruelty?

"It's a blessing you're alive," Bianca insisted.

His blindly loyal housekeeper had always been a rock he could count on. Now it seemed he was going to have to rely on her and her husband Angelo more than ever. "Can I trust you to keep the most important secret of your life?"

"You insult me with that question!"

"*Mi dispiace,* but it's vitally important none of this gets out, not even to the family. Something could leak to the paparazzi. No one must get wind of this until I'm ready for the world to know."

"No one will learn anything from us."

"*Grazie,* Bianca."

"What is it?"

"My plan is to fly to Positano in a few hours, but I won't be alone. I need you and Angelo to organize the staff and get rooms ready for two people who will be living with us."

"I'll see to everything immediately. It's good you're coming home where you can be waited on. This house has been empty too long."

"Get prepared to hear the patter of little feet from now on."

"Little feet?"

"*Si,* Bianca. A five-year-old boy named Jean-Cesar Priestley de Falcon." But for a slight difference in hue, he had Sarah's eyes.

After a pause, comprehension dawned on Bianca. She let out the gasp Cesar had been forced to hold back when Sarah had presented their son to him.

Exactly.

"His mother will be with us."

"Ah—"

Ah... Six years ago his housekeeper had been witness to the shape he had been in after the phone conversation with Sarah that had thrown him into a black void. No one but Bianca and Angelo could have put up with him back then.

"*A presto,* Bianca."

He hung up, his mind still on Sarah whose omission constituted an unforgivable sin in Cesar's mind, but he couldn't fault her for the name she'd given Johnny. Saying it out loud to the housekeeper had filled him with an inexplicable sense of pride. Cesar's parents wouldn't be able to contain their joy.

His brother, Luc, would be blown away to know Cesar had a son older than Luc's.

As for Cesar's best friend and cousin, Massimo was the only person who knew anything about Sarah. In a few days he would phone him in Guatemala and tell him the monumental news.

Until Cesar had seen the son of his flesh and Sarah's, he hadn't wanted to go on living...

Incredible to realize she had become pregnant without either of them realizing it. Of course she and Johnny were indispensable to each other. You didn't break up a mother and child.

If he wanted his son with him day and night, he had no choice but to marry her. For Johnny's sake Cesar was determined to make this wedding special enough that his son would always remember their first memories together with happiness.

The thought of being legally wed to a woman as deceitful as Sarah was anathema to him, but he had to admit she was an amazing mother.

Johnny might be his own spirit—he might have an innate charm all his own—he might possess the kind of good looks and intelligence any man would want in a son, but Johnny's excellent behavior and manners, his breeding, his politeness, his sweet sensitivity and kindness—all those things could be laid at the feet of the woman who'd raised him.

If Cesar were honest with himself, he could see in his son the things he'd loved about Sarah at seventeen.

When she'd first appeared in his hospital room, Cesar figured he was having an irreversible mental collapse, the kind you didn't survive. But after she'd come back in again, everything changed.

Within seconds of seeing that precious five-year-old face and looking into those mirrors of the soul staring at him in such rapt curiosity, Cesar had felt an energizing force surge through his nervous system bringing it back to breathtaking life.

"Mommy!" Johnny cried as Sarah entered the room once more, causing Cesar's gaze to swerve toward the door. He'd been waiting for her return so they could get the ceremony over with and fly away from this claustrophobic prison. She carried two medium-size suitcases.

He was still stunned at the change in her. In six years the enchanting girl he'd lost his head over had turned into a mature woman he hardly recognized without her silky dark hair hanging down her back.

With her standing there on those long shapely legs, he was forced to concede she'd grown into a voluptuous beauty. The birth of a baby did that for some women. It galled him to have to admit he couldn't take his eyes off her, particularly when he was appalled by what she'd done to him… To them…

Sarah felt Cesar's daunting scrutiny and trembled. "I'm sorry it took me so long."

"An hour and a half to be exact," he muttered.

"I know, but the line at the front desk took forever." She put the bags down against the wall.

"We're ready to go get married, Mommy."

When she lifted her head, her breath caught. Cesar had been helped to a wheelchair. But in the midnight-blue silk suit and impeccable white dress shirt he was wearing, all she saw was the gorgeous, dashing figure of the race car driver she'd fallen in love with years before.

No one seeing him like this could imagine him having an injury that prevented him from walking. In the left lapel he wore a white rose. The contrast of color against his fabulous olive skin and black hair set her pulse racing.

"Here, Mommy. This is for you." Johnny ran across the room to hand her a small paper box. Only then did she notice him dressed in a new dark blue suit and white shirt Cesar had arranged for him to wear. In the left lapel he, too, was wearing a white rosebud.

The sight caused her heart to swell. "Thank you, honey. Don't you look handsome!"

"Daddy and I look alike."

"You surely do." You're the two most beautiful men in the world.

She glanced down to see a corsage of white roses beneath the clear cellophane top. "How lovely!" she exclaimed as she drew off the cover.

"Daddy wants you to wear them."

Cesar wheeled himself over to her. "Lean over and I'll put it on you."

While he drew the corsage from the box, she did his bidding. Her heart was thudding so hard, she knew he could see it by the movement of the material covering her chest. Because the blood was thundering in her ears, he could probably hear it.

As he fastened the flowers to her shoulder, his deft, suntanned fingers brushed against her body. She closed her eyes tightly, afraid to breathe. Through the thin fabric, the heat of contact against her skin had set off an explosion. It sent out shock waves to every atom and corpuscle.

"Are you okay, Mommy?"

His child eyes didn't miss a trick.

"I'm fine."

"Then how now come your eyes are closed?"

"I—I didn't realize they were." She opened them only to discover Cesar's mere inches from hers. The mocking glint told her he knew exactly how his touch affected her. He knew how his hands and mouth and body had always driven her mad with desire.

"Let's go," he said seconds later in a deep, thick toned voice and put his hands on the wheels.

"I'm ready." Johnny stood behind him and helped push the wheelchair toward the door. Anyone else would think they were playing a game, that Cesar was pretending to take a ride to amuse his son. Sarah walked behind them. For her the moment was bittersweet to see Johnny helping his father.

On their way to the elevator they had to pass in front of a flank of hospital staff waiting to offer their congratulations to a man whose name and fame was renowned throughout Europe, particularly in Monaco and Italy. Everyone was in tears. Even the doctor. He sought Sarah's eyes and lifted two thumbs up to her in private salute.

Sarah noted the large number of security guards everywhere. It reminded her that the hospital was sitting on a story that would earn millions of dollars for the media once the public was informed.

Racing and royalty were a dynamite combination, but add the element of the paralyzed playboy bachelor who'd kept his wife and child hidden for six years, and the story would grow legs that marched around the world.

Soon they reached the second floor. The ornate interior of the small chapel surprised Sarah. Everything about Italy, from the style of the buildings and statues to the seductive quality of the language, thrilled her.

An old priest in formal robes urged the three of them forward. "Come closer," he said in English. Except for the hospital staff who stood in as witnesses, they had the chapel to themselves for the ceremony.

When they reached him, he leaned down with a smiling face to shake Johnny's hand. "I baptized your father after he was born. To think he has such a fine son to present on his wedding day. What's your name?"

"Je-Jean-Cesar Priestley de Falcon."

Fighting tears, Sarah cast a covert glance at Cesar. She thought his eyes looked suspiciously bright just then. Their son had said it pretty faultlessly for a five-year-old American boy who'd only had a few coaching lessons from his father in the last hour or so.

"Well Jean-Cesar, it's a pleasure to meet such a wonderful young man. I know you will always be a great comfort to him, especially now while he is recovering from his ordeal."

"Will you bless him so he can walk, Father?"

"I've already done that and will continue to pray to God for him. But it's also up to you, and your father, and your mother, to make the miracle happen."

His raisin dark eyes lifted to Sarah's. He studied her for a long moment and then they traveled to Cesar's. "A strong family is the greatest medicine on earth. Courage, my children, and you'll come out the conquerors. Let us pray."

Before she lowered her head, Sarah saw Johnny and his father bow their dark heads in obedience. Once the priest had offered up beautiful words of hope, he told Cesar to take her hand.

He reached across the arm of the wheelchair to grasp hers. The moment had an air of unreality as they exchanged vows to honor, love and cherish each other in sickness and health all the days of their lives. How many times had she dreamed of this very moment?

But under vastly different circumstances.

"I now pronounce you, Sarah Priestley and you, Cesar Villon de Falcon, husband and wife from this day forward. What God has joined together, let no man put asunder. In the name of the Father, and the Son and the Holy Spirit, Amen." He made the sign of the cross.

"Amen," Sarah whispered.

Johnny let out a big sigh. "Are you married now?"

"We are," Cesar muttered in his deep voice.

"Where's Mommy's ring?"

"At the villa."

"Oh." After pondering that answer he said, "Aren't you going to kiss each other?"

"Yes," Sarah spoke before Cesar could. To save him any embarrassment she leaned down and pressed her lips to his. The gesture made everything seem real enough to the onlookers. But

Sarah's heart shattered into pieces because it felt like she was kissing a cold, stone wall.

The second she lifted her head, Cesar grabbed Johnny and pulled him onto his lap. He turned and threw his arms around Cesar's neck. They clung to each other. Two dark curly heads pressed together. Sarah could hardly breathe for the emotions attacking her from all directions.

"You're officially my son now. We'll never be apart again." He kissed the top of his head. "Are you ready for that helicopter ride?"

"Yes."

The priest asked them to step to the back of the chapel where they needed to put their signatures to the marriage documents. When that was done, she shook hands with him. "Thank you, Father."

He turned her to the side away from Johnny and Cesar. "I've known your husband all his life. He guards his heart well." It appeared the priest had seen the truth of the situation with that kiss. "Be patient through the dark times ahead. One day the sun will come out."

Sarah wanted to have his faith, but the words "one day" plunged her to a new threshold of despair.

A group of hospital workers escorted them to another elevator that took everyone to the roof. At five-thirty in the evening, the heat from the sun was almost too much. She walked toward the medical helicopter where she watched an attendant help Johnny inside. Two other workers lifted Cesar.

One of the ground crew stowed her bags onboard while another man helped her inside and handed her the throwaway camera. He'd been the one to take pictures during the wedding ceremony. She thanked him before strapping herself in.

Cesar had put on a pair of sunglasses, reminding her of the many newspaper photos showing the dashing race car driver after another win, or walking along the street in company with an international beauty.

He looked fabulous in his wedding clothes. Before he caught her staring, she quickly flicked her gaze to Johnny. Even without their matching colors, anyone seeing them together would immediately notice the unmistakable resemblance.

"Are you excited, honey?"

"Yup."

His smile didn't fool her. He was scared, but he'd never admit it in front of his father.

Sarah had ridden in a helicopter with her parents when they'd gone to Hawaii, but it was much smaller and built for sightseeing.

The pilot and copilot nodded to her, then the blades began to rotate. At this point she knew Johnny was ready to jump out of his skin. So was she, but for an entirely different reason. Cesar must have sensed his fear. The minute there was liftoff, she saw him put a hand over Johnny's on the armrest.

"This is how it felt the first time I drove around a track in a race car, *mio piccolo.* After a minute I got used to the sensation. Keep your eye on me and everything's going to be fine."

Johnny took his father's advice and looked up at him. His sweet little expression so full of trust in spite of his apprehension, spoke to Sarah's heart.

In a few minutes they'd left Rome and were traveling in a southerly direction. At his father's urging, Johnny finally dared to glance out the window. The sight was so spectacular he forgot to be afraid.

For the next half hour everyone in the helicopter was treated to his bursts of excitement shouted between comments only a child would think to say. The look of fatherly pride in Cesar's eyes, the sound of his low laughter as he responded to his son's unique observations was something Sarah would cherish forever.

The helicopter followed the Amalfi Coast, renowned as one of the most glorious regions in all Italy. Years ago Cesar had borrowed her laptop to show her a map of the whole area including the picturesque town of Positano. He'd pointed to the spot where his villa was located, giving her a graphic description of what to expect when she vacationed with him there.

But nothing prepared her for the breathtaking view assaulting her eyes as they drew closer. The town spilled over the flowering hillside like it had tumbled from the top to the blue bay below, leaving the pink and white, square-shaped Moorish houses almost on top of each other.

"Mommy— See all those cars? They look like tiny bugs marching to war."

She was so captivated by the town's beauty, it took her a minute to realize Johnny was talking about the bumper to bumper traffic lined up along the coastal road as far as the eye could see. Nothing seemed to be moving.

"Good heavens! It looks exactly like that, honey."

"The locals try not to drive here during the summer months," the pilot commented. "This is the only way to see everything."

"You're right," she whispered, uncomfortably aware of Cesar's silence. No doubt he was thinking of the thousands of moments he'd missed out on by not being with his son.

With those dark lenses, she couldn't tell if he was looking at her or not. But she didn't need to see his eyes to know he felt something deeper than hatred for what she'd done.

"Where's our villa, Daddy?" Johnny was a fast learner.

Cesar leaned closer to him and pointed. "See that pink one on top of the hill?"

Johnny pressed his nose to the window. "It looks like a palace!"

It did. Even down to the number of security men to guard Cesar's privacy.

A low chuckle escaped Cesar's throat. "It's too small for a real palace. Do you like it?"

"I love it!"

Images started to flood her mind in contemplation of what it would have been like if she'd joined him in this paradise six years ago. She wouldn't have been able to hold back telling him she was expecting his baby. And then what?

She hadn't had an answer to that question back then, but she did now. Cesar was overjoyed. His instant transformation from bachelor to father was total. It had happened in a twinkling of Johnny's worshipful gray-blue eyes focused on his daddy.

"We're ready to land," the pilot informed them.

Cesar sat back, but she noticed he'd grasped Johnny's hand and held on to it until after the helicopter had touched ground and the whirring of the rotors slowed down. Who needed whom the most?

The helipad formed part of a small clinic on the east side of the slope. Outside staff took over to help transfer Cesar from the helicopter to a waiting ambucar. Sarah thanked the pilot before she and Johnny climbed inside after him.

She gave Cesar a furtive glance, noting the way his jaw had hardened. After being touted the king of speed for years, to now require assistance from trained health care workers would drain every ounce of that indomitable will just to accept help.

On his own level Johnny showed an uncanny understanding of what was going on inside his father. He patted his smooth shaven cheek. "Are you okay, Daddy?"

Cesar rubbed the back of Johnny's neck. "With you here, how could I be anything else?"

Sarah forced herself to look out of the window. *Keep saying that, Cesar. Keep believing it and you'll get through this stronger than ever.*

Before she and Johnny had made their appearance, Cesar had planned to leave the hospital. But he hadn't anticipated returning home with his own child in tow. This had to be a surreal experience for him.

The driver started up the car. Within seconds they were winding their way along an impossibly narrow lane that climbed past several luxury villas.

After negotiating a hairpin turn, the car slowed down and pulled into a private driveway half hidden by massive overhangs of flowers in shades from shocking pinks to blues and purples. The gate opened to allow them entrance. Soon they drew to a stop at the rear of the pink villa they'd seen from the air.

"We're home," Cesar declared.

"Hooray!" Johnny scrambled from the car, too excited to sit still any longer. Sarah climbed out after him. Perfume from the flowers assailed her senses.

The next few minutes became a blur as the hospital attendant produced a wheelchair and pushed him through a flower-filled arbor to a breathtaking inner courtyard surrounding a rectangular pool.

Johnny had been right. The villa was like a palace.

Once the attendant left to go back to the car, an older woman and man, both with dark blond hair, came running from the portico and converged on Cesar to welcome him back. From their hugs and cries, Sarah could tell his staff adored him.

He removed his sunglasses and reached for Johnny, pulling him onto his lap. "Bianca? Angelo?" he spoke in English. "This is my son, Johnny. Johnny, meet the Carlonis."

"Hi!"

His bright young voice was like a ray of sunshine.

"Such a beautiful boy!" Bianca cried. Sounds of pure delight poured out of the wiry older woman as she leaned over to kiss him on both cheeks.

Angelo, built like a bull, beamed at him. "You look like a young Cesar."

"That's what the pilot said." Obviously Johnny was thrilled over the comparison.

"The Carlonis have lived here for years and take care of me and the house."

"Mommy and I will take care of you."

Cesar kissed the top of his head. "How about we all take care of each other. Sarah?" he called to her unexpectedly without looking at her, almost as if she were excess baggage.

On trembling legs she approached to shake hands with his staff.

Still addressing the others he said, "Meet my wife, Sarah Priestley, now de Falcon."

Her name seemed to mean something to the housekeeper whose black eyes darted to Sarah with an unsmiling expression.

"We were just married in the hospital chapel. No one is to know I'm home yet. Until tomorrow I want everything kept quiet. *Capisce?*"

"*Si,* Cesar," Bianca murmured. Her husband simply nodded.

"Johnny? If you want to come with me and Angelo, Bianca will take care of your mother. Then we'll eat on the terrace."

"The cook has dinner ready," the housekeeper informed them.

Johnny cocked his head. "You have a cook?"

His father smiled at him. "Now you do, too. Her name is Juliana. She'll fix you anything you like."

At those words Johnny jumped up and down with excitement. He seemed perfectly happy to go with his father. If he felt any separation anxiety, he was hiding it well.

"I'll see you in a minute, honey."

"Okay."

Bianca turned to her. "Come with me, Signora Falcon."

She reached for Sarah's bag and led her beneath another portico to the end of the pool. They passed through a set of French doors into a guest bedroom done in shades of aqua and oyster with a modern, en suite bathroom. Every amenity had been provided.

A striped silk spread on the queen-size bed,

plus matching stripes on the chairs and love seat made it a beautiful room that reflected the turquoise of the pool.

"This is lovely." She looked around. "Where does that door lead?"

"To the hallway."

"I see. Where have you put Johnny?"

"In his father's suite at the other end of the villa."

Was this Cesar's or Bianca's idea of how things should work?

The housekeeper was civil enough, yet Sarah detected hostility coming from her. Like a possessive mother who turned on anyone hurting her child, she clearly blamed Sarah for this situation and intended to make it up to Cesar.

But Bianca didn't know Johnny. He was still too young and vulnerable to handle this arrangement. Since Sarah didn't want to do anything to alienate the housekeeper further, she would discuss this with Cesar when they were alone.

"Dinner will be served on the west terrace. After you're settled, walk down the hall to the foyer and go straight out the French doors."

"Thank you, Bianca."

With a closed expression, the housekeeper disappeared from the room.

Sarah was having to function one minute at a time. No one at the villa welcomed her here, least of all Cesar. She was only tolerated because she was Johnny's mother. It was something she would have to get used to in order to survive.

She freshened up in the bathroom, changing into white Capri pants and a filmy yellow and white print blouson top. Once she'd slipped into Italian leather sandals, she started for the foyer.

The promise to make a quick call to her parents would have to keep until she went to bed.

Yesterday Sarah had phoned to let them know she and Johnny had arrived safely in Rome. Naturally they had asked her to let them know the outcome of today's hospital visit. They'd be shocked to discover she was already married. Her sister, Elaine, would be elated.

Since they'd never approved of her keeping Johnny a secret from Cesar, she knew they'd be relieved the truth was finally out. For their grandson's sake they'd be happy a marriage had taken place.

But they had no comprehension of Cesar's true

state of mind. Under the circumstances Sarah was glad to put off talking to them. For the moment she had no desire to go into detail over the precarious nature of the situation with Cesar. That could wait until she'd gotten her bearings.

After applying some lotion, she took a fortifying breath and went in search of Johnny. She needed the warmth of her darling boy to ward off the chill Bianca had brought into the room.

As Sarah came to find out, the villa was an architectural wonder of latticed passageways forming a structure like an ornate tiara. She moved past more bedrooms to the other part of the house. Fabulous oriental rugs covered the marble floors. Throughout the dining and living room she feasted her eyes on huge brass urns filled with flowering plants. Venetian glass mirrors and wall sconces with tapered candles graced the walls. Against a backdrop that whispered of a sultan's palace, the blend of European furnishings in shades of pale to deep rose silk and damask enchanted her.

She found it difficult to reconcile that a man of the twenty-first century who loved speed and pushed the limits of the latest race car technology to the extreme came from a home steeped in this kind of timeless splendor. His environment and interests proved to be as complex as Cesar himself. A man whose dark hair and sun-kissed skin had captured her attention the first time she'd laid eyes on him.

Tall and buff with eyes that flashed a shimmery silver, she'd never met anyone remotely like him. Without his exceptional skill behind the wheel at an early age, catapulting him to stardom, their worlds would never have collided in Monterey.

He possessed sophistication and intelligence that put him on a level above the other males of her acquaintance, and she had fallen so deeply in love with him. Six years of separation hadn't changed her feelings. If anything, Johnny's birth had only intensified her need for Cesar. He'd spoiled her for anyone else.

Almost to the terrace now, she caught sight of him in the wheelchair. He was pointing out something to their animated son who stood next to him at the wrought-iron railing.

Cesar's exceptional looks and personality made him attractive to men and women alike. She drew closer, noting that Johnny was no exception. Love for his father shone from his eyes. He saw beyond the wheelchair to the man, making no comparisons or judgments. His pure devotion was exactly what Cesar needed.

Even though Sarah felt like she'd walked into a fiery furnace coming to Italy, she knew it had been the right thing to do. Only time would tell if she could withstand the heat long enough to get past Cesar's bitter rancor.

Johnny saw her first and flew across the terrace to hug her. She'd never been so happy to feel those arms around her. Both he and Cesar had changed into casual shirts and trousers.

"Come and look, Mommy!" As Johnny grasped her hand and pulled her toward the railing overhung with masses of lavender bougainvillea, she felt Cesar's eyes on her. But his punitive gaze couldn't prevent the gasp that escaped her lips.

Surely no spot on earth equaled the sight before her eyes. The villa sat perched on the pinnacle of a steep mount. Once long ago Cesar had told her Positano was gifted with a dramatic beauty that drew the adulation of the world. Now she knew what he meant.

The fragrance of the sultry air, the breathtaking view of a brilliant blue sea and sky separated by the charming town built into the cliffs presented a paradise beyond any words she could conjure.

Johnny pointed toward the ocean. "See those islands?"

She nodded.

"They're called the Galli islands. Daddy said Sirens used to live there and were dangerous. What's a Siren?"

"Didn't he tell you?"

"He said to ask you because you know all about them."

Heat stained her cheeks.

Refusing to look at Cesar she said, "They were imaginary women with birdlike bodies who sang when ships went by."

"How come they were dangerous?"

"Because their songs were so beautiful, they made men want to jump ship and swim over to them," Cesar supplied. "But the men died in the water trying to reach them."

A look of concentration had broken out on Johnny's face. "They shouldn't have sailed near them."

"You're right, *figlio mio.* Unfortunately they learned their lesson too late."

Anger swamped her.

Cesar had made certain he'd escaped her clutches without being swallowed in the depths of the sea. As far as she was concerned he'd gotten his legends mixed up.

If anything she could liken him to the mythical Apollo who raced around mating with many women, never settling down to one. She would love to say something about that to him, but not in front of Johnny.

"It's a pretend story, honey. Come on—let's sit down and eat."

They joined Cesar at the round glass table where a maid named Concetta had just served their food.

"Mommy? Bianca said Juliana made mac and cheese just for me."

"Well aren't you a lucky boy. That's one of your favorite meals."

He nodded. "What's yours, Daddy?"

"I like it, too."

From the way Johnny sat on the chair swinging his legs back and forth beneath the seat, she could tell he was happy.

"Hey, Daddy?" he said after he'd made inroads on his dinner. "What are we going to do after we eat?"

"Your father just got out of the hospital, honey. Since it's been a long day, we're all going to bed early."

Cesar shot her a warning glance before his gaze switched to Johnny. "How would you like to see my gym?"

"Where is it?"

"Down the hall encircling the far side of the pool."

"You mean in *our* house?" Clearly he was surprised.

"*Si, piccolo mio.* It's in a big room where I work out to stay in shape between races."

"What have you got in it?"

"Well, there's a barbell bench, an incline bench, a decline bench, free weights, dumbbells, a cable machine, a treadmill and a bicycle."

"Whoa— Can I work out with you?"

"We'll do some curls tonight."

"What are those?"

"An exercise. We'll work with the dumbbells to strengthen our biceps."

"What are biceps?"

"These." He patted Johnny's upper arm muscle. "Pretty soon yours will be bigger than Carson's."

"His are kind of little."

"I thought so."

"But you haven't seen Carson before. You're funny, Daddy. I love you."

"I love you, too." He took another bite of macaroni. "Tomorrow we'll go shopping for some toys, and afterward we'll take a swim. It'll feel good after the heat."

"I can't swim very well, but I can dive off the side if Mommy catches me."

"I'm here to catch you now."

CHAPTER FOUR

SARAH had picked up Cesar's warning signal loud and clear. *It's my turn,* it said. She knew. She wouldn't dream of taking this time away from him for anything.

After the black mental state he'd been in at the hospital, she was overjoyed to see that Johnny's presence had sparked fresh life into his psyche. But she was afraid he was going to overdo it and burn out too fast.

Twelve hours ago she and Johnny had just stepped into a taxi to go to the hospital. So much had happened since then, she could hardly process the fact that she was a married woman. From now on she would be referred to as Signora de Falcon, wife of the great Cesar Villon who was a household name to those following the Formula 1 circuit.

When she thought of how his parents and

family would react to the news, she trembled with apprehension. His mother would secretly despise her for keeping her grandson from his father all this time.

She tried to imagine how she would feel if someday Johnny had a baby with a woman who didn't tell him about it for years and years. The pain and the hurt for him would be devastating—incalculable.

Yet she was expecting Cesar to be understanding of her reasons for keeping all knowledge of Johnny from him until now.

Her hands clutched the sides of her chair seat. How could she have done this to him? To her little boy? Look how the two of them had already bonded!

While she sat there riddled with pain for her crime, she made a vow to do everything in her power to make up for those lost years. From here on out Cesar's wishes and needs would come first.

No doubt he was hoping she'd leave the table so he could be alone to enjoy his first dinner with his own son, an experience she'd shared with Johnny thousands of times. That much she could do for him.

She quickly finished the rest of her meal, then got up from her chair. Avoiding Cesar's eyes she said, "If you will excuse me, I have a few phone calls to make. Have fun you two."

"Who would you be phoning at four o'clock in the morning California time?"

Cesar's question stopped her cold.

"That's right," she laughed nervously, not only from surprise because she'd forgotten about the time difference, but because Cesar might think she was going to phone Mick. After what she'd told him about them just being friends, he had every reason to be suspicious.

She felt his half shuttered gaze examine her inch by inch before he said, "When I asked Bianca to get the rooms ready earlier, she assumed that in my condition I would need my bedroom to myself. But as Johnny pointed out, Carson's mommy and daddy sleep in the same room. So feel free to move your things to my bedroom now."

The command was implicit. "When you reach the foyer, turn left. It's the room at the end of the hall."

No matter how Cesar couched the words, he

wanted them sleeping together. Even if it was for Johnny's sake, a thrill of excitement coursed through her body.

"My room is right next to yours and Daddy's, Mommy." She could tell their son's fears had been taken away by one word from his father who could fix anything and make everything better.

Her first instinct was to ask Johnny if he wanted to help her move her suitcase to the other part of the house, but she caught herself in time. Unfortunately old habits didn't die right off the bat. She and Johnny had been a twosome for so long, it felt strange to relinquish any responsibility to someone else. Except that Cesar wasn't just someone.

He was Johnny's other parent who'd embraced fatherhood without missing a heartbeat. It had been instant adoration on both their parts. Johnny wanted to be with his father, which meant more free time for Sarah, who didn't really want it.

He'd been her whole world from the moment she'd conceived. Now she would be sharing him the way two parents did in a normal household.

"I'll see you two a little later then."

Without giving Johnny a chance to ask questions she might not be able to answer, she left the terrace and hurried through the villa to her room.

She'd only been in there long enough to change clothes and wash her face, so there wasn't much to gather or tidy. Within a few minutes she had retraced her steps to the foyer with her suitcase and turned left. The tall, ornately carved wood doors at the end had to be the entry to the master suite.

When she opened them she stepped into a dreamy world no doubt created to help Cesar relax after a race. Like the guest bedroom she'd just left, it bordered the pool. However, this breathtaking room with its king-size bed was much larger. Two framed Michelanglo drawings hung above it. A huge hand-painted French armoire in antique white stood against one wall. There was an ornate couch and love seat. They faced an exquisitely carved fireplace.

Two Louis XV striped chairs were placed at either side of a white marble table. The furniture was upholstered in cream silk with strong accents of café-au-lait woven into the decor, some in stripes, others in an all-over print. Pots of creamy roses completed the enchanting picture.

Opposite the bed, floor to ceiling glass doors opened onto another terrace, offering a spectacular view of the ocean.

Putting her suitcase down, she stepped outside and wandered over to the railing. The beauty from this angle was so indescribable, it hurt. She stood there for a long time drinking it in before tearing herself from the view to explore the rest of the suite.

One door led to Johnny's smaller bedroom with its queen-size bed and en suite bathroom. The lemon-yellow and white decor throughout was a delight.

Behind another door she discovered the luxuriously appointed master bathroom with an oversize jetta tub. A third set of double doors opened into Cesar's study containing state-of-the-art computer equipment.

This room belonged to the race car driver. All his trophies and awards, pictures—everything was here, modestly tucked away from the world's prying eyes.

Where many great sports stars might make their whole house into a shrine, he'd chosen this quiet spot to keep all the mementos precious to him. Cesar had always represented the epitome of class to her. Now she knew why.

Take away his aristocratic background and you would still have the same marvelous man. Deep down he was a very private person who, though he thrived on competition, was amazingly humble about his colossal successes.

It was the race that challenged him. He had an inner drive that provoked him to pit himself against the odds. That's what was important, not the accolades that followed. She blamed the media for the hype about him. Most of it, if not all, was untrue.

In his hospital room this morning, the violence of his emotions revealed a side of his nature few people would ever glimpse. But she'd seen into his soul and discovered a man who wanted his son more than any prize his sport could bestow on him. She was also convinced that if he hadn't been involved in that accident, he still would have had exactly the same reaction when she introduced him to his son in California.

She saw a hunger in him. The longing to be a father must have always been there. He'd never denied that he wanted to have a family one day, just that he was putting it off until he could commit property. But destiny had decreed that day to come sooner than he'd expected, changing the lives of three people forever.

A sob rose in her throat. She sank down on the bed, running her hand over the luminous cream bedspread.

"Darling Cesar—if there had to be an accident, why didn't it happen to me? Not you, my love. Not you."

A searing ache passed through her body. Suddenly she felt a hand shaking her arm. "Mommy? What's wrong?"

Johnny had slipped into the room so quietly, she hadn't heard him.

"Daddy? Mommy's crying."

"Maybe she's upset because she thought I forgot to give her the wedding ring I promised."

Before turning her head toward them, Sarah hurriedly tried to repair the damage from her crying spell, but nothing escaped Cesar's notice. He'd maneuvered his wheelchair next to the dresser to pull something from the drawer. When he returned to the side of the bed, his penetrating eyes examined her wet cheeks, showing her no mercy.

"See this ruby, Johnny?" He opened his palm

to display a ring. "General Napoleon Bonaparte brought it back from his Egyptian campaign. It's called Alexandria's heart."

Johnny picked it up to look at it. "It's really pretty."

"This stone has been in the Varano family for generations. After my mother inherited it, she had it set in gold. On my twenty-first birthday, she gave it to me. She told me I should present this to the woman I wanted to marry."

So his parents hadn't decided his choice of bride after all…

"Give me your left hand, Sarah."

One of the famous Varano jewels—

Little did Cesar's mother realize it would end up on the finger of a little nobody from the States who'd been so careless with her son's heart as to keep his child from him.

But no matter how ludicrous this was she'd made a promise to put his interests first. Every gesture on this red-letter day had a symbolic purpose and would make an indelible impression on Johnny's mind. Already his father was teaching him how things worked when you were born a Varano and a Falcon.

She shifted her position around on the bed to make it easier before extending her hand. Using his left hand to steady her wrist, he slid it onto her ring finger with his right. His sure touch shot fire up her arm. Even after he'd relinquished his hold on her, she still felt his imprint stealing through the rest of her sensitized body.

When she looked down, the facets of the large, fiery red stone had caught the soft light from the lamps placed at either side of the bed. She found it apropos that it looked very much to her like her own bleeding heart.

Johnny stared up at her. "Do you feel better now?"

"Much." She reached out to hug him, aware her new husband was waiting for some kind of response. Over Johnny's shoulder she said, "Thank you, Cesar. It's priceless. I just hope and pray nothing ever happens to it." She was terrified of losing an irreplaceable family heirloom.

"If you do, so be it. When Johnny finds the woman he wants to marry, there are other jewels at the ducal palace in Parma for him to choose from." Beneath his mocking tone she knew Cesar expected her to carry on his family's tradition, but he didn't place any faith in her ability to deliver.

"Jewels—can I look at them, Daddy?"

"Of course. We'll take a trip to visit my cousin Maximilliano and his wife Greer. They have a little boy who looks a lot like you named Carlo. Of course he's younger. You're the *oldest* of all your cousins."

A smile broke out on Johnny's face. Evidently the idea pleased him. "Do I have a lot of cousins?"

Cesar nodded. "My other cousin Nicolas and his wife Piper just had triplets."

"Triplets—"

"That means three babies at once," Sarah explained. She couldn't imagine it.

"Whoa."

"Two girls and a boy. Lety, Carolina and Fernando." This from Cesar. "And I have another cousin Massimo who's a new daddy. He'll be coming to visit us soon."

Massimo… Sarah knew that name well. There'd been moments in the last six years when she'd been tempted to call him and ask his advice. But every time she'd reached for the phone she'd lost her nerve and couldn't do it. If Cesar ever found out she'd told Massimo the news first, that would have made things so much worse.

"What's his baby's name?"

"Nicky di Rocche. His mommy Julie is from Sonoma, California."

"Hey, we've been there, haven't we, Mommy."

Her eyes met Cesar's for a breathless moment before she said, "Yes. What a remarkable coincidence."

"Indeed," he murmured, as if to say there was a lot Johnny had missed out on by being deprived of his father.

Sarah tore her eyes away. So many names and children Johnny couldn't remember. But she had a suspicion that Cesar had deliberately gone into detail to make her feel worse about what she'd done to him by depriving him of *his* son.

"My auntie Elaine is going to have another baby."

Cesar cocked his dark head. "I remember her. Does she still have red hair?"

"Yes. And she's afraid her baby will, too."

"Why is she afraid?"

"Cos kids will tease it."

"Sometimes children aren't nice, are they?"

"Nope. Carson wasn't nice when he called me a crybaby."

"I agree."

"Did anybody ever hurt your feelings?"

He sent Sarah a crushing regard. "Yes," came a sound from his throat resembling a hiss.

She had trouble swallowing. "Johnny? It's getting late. You need to have a bath and go to bed."

"Okay."

"I'll turn on the water."

She jumped off the bed, anxious to get away from Cesar. But when she headed for Johnny's room, he told her to wait. "Let him take a bath in our tub. He can swim in it."

"*Swim—*" He squealed in delight and ran into the master bath to investigate. In two seconds he'd stripped and climbed over the edge of the tub to get in. Soon he was demonstrating his splashing prowess.

Sarah felt Cesar's presence behind her as she knelt down to wash Johnny's hair.

"Look, Daddy— I can hold my breath." He leaned over and kept his head under the water while she rinsed his curls. When he raised it up again with a triumphant smile, he resembled one of the those appealing, mischievous Italian cherubs she'd seen in the chapel. He looked like Cesar.

She quaked inside.

"I'll get your jammies."

"Let me," Cesar forestalled her. "Which ones do you want me to bring, *piccolo mio?* The dinosaurs or the superheroes?"

"A… T-rex!"

"Tyrannosaurus Rex it is."

He wheeled around with a dexterity that proclaimed him an athlete's athlete and left the bathroom. By the time he returned with their son's pajamas and toothbrush, Johnny had climbed out of the tub. He insisted on drying himself with one of the big fluffy tan and white striped towels. Cesar smiled and handed him his jammies. When he'd pulled everything on, he helped himself to Cesar's toothpaste and brushed his teeth.

"I'm ready to go to bed now." His eyes sought his father's. "Will you come in while I say my prayers?"

"Try and stop me." Cesar made a pretend fist below Johnny's chin.

"Let me do that."

Johnny imitated everything his father did. Like

a sponge soaking up water, he was constantly absorbing every action and nuance.

Sarah preceded them into the bedroom where their son would be sleeping from now on. She turned down the covers and put the miniature model of his daddy's faucon by the pillow along with a couple of small dinosaurs he'd brought with him.

In a minute the two of them entered the room. Sarah perched on the edge of the bed. Johnny ran over and got down on his knees. Cesar glided over to them. Giving his dad one more glance to make sure he was there he began.

"Dear Heavenly Father— I love my daddy. Thanks for letting us get married. Thanks for not letting me be too scared in the helicopter. Bless Nana and Papa and my grandma and grandpa and all my cousins. Bless Daddy's legs to get better. Bless Mommy so she'll stop crying. Amen."

"Amen." Sarah got up from the bed. "Excuse me for a minute."

While Cesar's gaze followed her from the room, he reached for Johnny. Emotion gripped him so hard he had trouble speaking. He glimpsed the black racecar that was no more. Sarah had placed it next to a triceratops and a T-Rex. Those little toys that made up his child's world. .

"I love you, Johnny. You've made me happier than I've been in my whole life."

"Me, too."

"Tell me something. Does your mother cry a lot?"

"Yes, cos she loves you so much."

Cesar's eyes closed tightly.

"But she doesn't think I can hear her. I wish she wouldn't," he said wistfully.

"It isn't fun when our mommies cry, is it."

"Nope. Does your mommy cry a lot?"

Probably too much. "I know she cries sometimes."

"Because she's afraid you'll crash, huh."

He patted the boy's sturdy back. "Well she doesn't have to worry about that anymore."

"Cos you had a big crash."

"Bigger than I expected."

Johnny picked up the car and looked at it. "When you get better, are you going to race again?"

His child's naiveté was a bittersweet revelation. "No. I'll be home from now on to enjoy my son."

"I'm glad." After a pause, "Daddy? If I get scared tonight, can I come in your room?"

A smile broke out on his lips. "Where else would you go?" He stroked the damp curls back off his forehead. "But if we leave one of the lamps on, maybe you won't get nervous."

"Thanks." He pressed his soft lips to Cesar's cheek, then crawled into bed pulling the covers over him. "Daddy? Do you want to see my scrap-book before you go to bed?"

"I didn't know you had one."

"I've had it a long time. Mommy helped me make it. I'll get it." After letting go of the car, he got back out of bed and hurried over to the chair where Sarah had put his suitcase. Once he'd undone the locks, he pulled it out and ran back to his side. "Here."

At the sight of it, a tight band constricted Cesar's breathing. With hands not quite steady he opened the cover and came face-to-face with a photograph of himself that Sarah had taken when he was just twenty-four. Nine years of history… It went back a long way.

She'd been seventeen at the time, already a ravishing American beauty. Until they'd started talking at the Priestley home, he'd thought she was older. Then her father walked over to introduce them and put Cesar in the know. He couldn't have made his point any clearer if he'd said, "Hands off."

Her young age and the name Priestley made her untouchable, which was a good thing because he'd been tempted and Edward Priestley had known it.

In the picture Cesar wore a T-shirt with his sponsor's logo and a pair of tight jeans. His hair was longer back than. It was shocking to see how cocky he had been, swaggering around in front of the camera with his trophy in the background, showing off for this girl-woman whose sweetness and beauty called to him like the Siren to Ulysses.

While he looked closer at the picture, Johnny poured over it with him. The idiotic grin on Cesar's face, put there by his first world championship win, made him look drunk with life. Those stars in his eyes were the same stars he saw in Johnny's right now.

"Can I see that trophy?"

"I'll show you everything tomorrow."

"You have a whole bunch, right?"

"Quite a few." But he'd give his soul to have had these years with Johnny instead. Years when a son and father needed each other. Tears stung his eyes. Damn you to hell, Sarah Priestley…de Falcon.

The picture staring back from the page mocked him.

Back then Cesar had felt immortal, ready to smash every previously set racing record. Standing there, he hadn't been capable of imagining the day coming when he wouldn't be able to pose for photo ops on his own two strong legs.

With a trembling hand he turned the page. There was a picture taken of him and Sarah with her family that same night.

"That's Nana and Papa, and Auntie Elaine and Mommy!"

He cleared his throat. "I can see that." Memories flooded his mind. "Did you know the Priestley name has a very important history?"

"It does?"

"Yes. Somewhere way back in your family another Priestley invented a machine to make carbonated water."

Johnny frowned in puzzlement. "What's that?"

"What's your favorite drink?"

"Milk."

Cesar laughed. "Besides milk?"

"Orange soda."

"You're part Italian all right. We Italians love our orange soda. It's made with carbonated water. All sparkling sodas are. That's why your grandfather runs the Quenchers Company now."

"I didn't know that. Who told you?"

"Your mommy."

She'd told Cesar a lot of things that first night. He had to admit there'd been an instant rapport between them, surprising in a woman so much younger than himself. A teenager with enough beauty and charm to lure him back to the Priestley home whenever he flew to the States for a race.

"Papa Priestley says you're the best driver in the world."

And the biggest bastard who ever lived for impregnating his daughter.

"I'm afraid not anymore, *mon fils*."

He helped Johnny get back in to bed and put the covers over him, then he moved on to another page. Thus began a journey into the past. His life unfurled before him in chronological order.

There were many shots of him and Sarah on the surf, or sailing on her father's boat.

One picture leaped out at him. It was the Inn along the Big Sur where they'd spent that glorious night. The two of them looked so damn happy it hit him in the gut, making it difficult to breathe.

She'd chronicled his career, leaving nothing out. Every race, every win. All of it documented. Some photo shots from magazines and tabloids had caught him celebrating with various dazzling females and celebrities at favorite jet-set night clubs around the world.

Others featured him standing by a newly won trophy with his parents and brother after the Monaco Grand Prix, or at Monza in Italy with his second cousin and best friend, Massimo.

Sarah had included everything. She'd even found pictures taken of him with his cousins, all of them older. Yet that one unforgettable night with her had produced a son who was the oldest of all his little cousins. Johnny was the most satisfying child he could ever have imagined.

His gaze left the pictures to look at his son who'd finally fallen asleep with his cheek lying on the car. He carefully removed it and put it on the bedside table with the dinosaurs. After such a long, eventful day in his young life, it was no wonder he'd passed out.

Earlier in the morning Cesar had suffered two shocks from which he didn't think he would ever recover. He'd honestly thought he was hallucinating when he'd heard Sarah's voice and saw her standing there like a beautiful frightened doe in the headlights.

After waiting years to hear from her without one damn word, for her to have come in the hospital room at his lowest ebb, he'd understood for the first time how someone could commit a crime of passion.

Who would have dreamed that after driving her out of the hospital room with his raging invective, she'd be right back with the son they'd created together? Their perfect child. Jean-Cesar…

Sarah was right. His mother would be crazy about her little Giovanni. Cesar knew his parents were suffering over his paralysis. Knowing their pain, he'd kept them away, unable to bear seeing it in their loving eyes. He couldn't deal with that yet.

Luc understood. He'd almost lost his leg in

a ski tram accident a few years ago. The despair had almost driven him mad. Olivia had changed all that.

Cesar's hands flattened on the arms of the wheelchair. Once his family heard the news, there was going to be celebrating at the Falcon estate in Monaco. One look at Johnny and joy would mitigate their anguish for him. He'd phone them in a little while.

Right now he wanted to stay here and try to comprehend the wonder of his boy's reality. After Cesar was certain his wife had gone to sleep, he would ask Angelo to help him get in to bed.

Not quite the picture of two lovers on fire for each other, is it Sarah?

CHAPTER FIVE

SARAH stood hidden at the doorway to Johnny's room studying Cesar's profile. She'd been watching and listening the whole time. An unseen hand squeezed her heart to see his head thrown back with his arm covering his eyes.

Cesar—

She turned away and removed the robe over her nightgown before getting into their bed. When he finally came in to the room, she wanted him to believe she was unconscious to the world. Sarah loved him so much, his condition would never matter to her. In fact she loved him more because of it. But without the love on his part, the situation was repugnant to him.

She had to come to terms with the fact that he despised the very thought of sleeping in the same bed with her. Only for Johnny's sake would he steel himself to go through the motions and pretend they were a typical, happily married couple.

In that regard Cesar was displaying the same heroic fighting nature that had catapulted him to racing stardom and made him a beloved sports hero in the eyes of millions.

Everyone well intentioned or not wanted a piece of him. When the paparazzi got their first photos of Johnny accompanying the dashing man in the wheelchair, the relationship between them unmistakable, a whole new wave of public sentiment would spread.

How could it not? To see two utterly handsome men, one little, one big, enjoying each other's company as only a father and son could do.

She may have handled everything else wrong with Cesar, but with Johnny's watchful eyes and thoughts going into the making of the scrapbook to honor his father, she'd given Cesar a priceless gift he couldn't reject.

Before she turned out the lamp on her side of the bed, she placed Johnny's baby book on Cesar's pillow. Another gift assembled from those very first moments following their baby's birth up to last week when she'd put in a picture of him posing next to Carson with their soccer team. All of it to help his father catch up on the years he'd missed with his son.

Elaine had taken dozens of those first photos in the hospital room. Pictures of the nursery, Sarah's doctor, the family taking turns holding the new little bundle…

Bless you, Elaine.

Having done all she could for tonight, Sarah turned away from his side of the bed and pulled the covers around her head. With the air-conditioning on to shut out the intense heat of the day, they actually felt good.

When Cesar was convinced Johnny wouldn't wake up, he wheeled himself out of the room and through the villa. Knowing Sarah was getting ready for bed, he wanted to put as much distance as possible between them. He soon found himself on the terrace.

Like the sheerest bridal veil, twilight had fallen upon the face of Positano. It was the time of night when anything Cesar was feeling seemed to be magnified a hundredfold. Awash with emotions he couldn't ignore, he realized it was time to contact his parents. Though the doctor would have given them updates, he had orders not to let them know Cesar had left the hospital.

But now that he was a father, it was as if he'd been given second sight. How come it had taken something this earthshaking for him to understand what a selfish bastard he'd been to shut them out? Since his decision to race cars, he'd put them through so much hell, they deserved to know before anyone else that he was no longer the bachelor they'd been worrying about all these years.

Without wasting any more time, he pulled out his cell phone to call them. They'd be in bed. His father answered after the first ring, which meant he'd been waiting. He would have seen Cesar's name on his caller ID.

"Mon cher fils—"

Cesar had to clear his throat. "Papa."

"Grace à Dieu!" He could hear his mother crying the same thing in the background.

"I'm sorry I haven't phoned before now. I couldn't. Forgive me."

"There's nothing to forgive. We understand." They always did. "What's important is that you're alive!"

He hadn't thought so until yesterday morning when he'd heard the shocking words, "Honey? This is your daddy."

"I realize it's late, Papa, but I wanted you to know I'm back in Positano. I can hear maman asking questions. Tell her I'm starting my physical therapy."

"That's the best news, *mon fils,* but you can't be expected to get through this alone. We'll be flying there tomorrow to help you."

Tomorrow would be too soon. Cesar needed another day to get into a routine with his son before the family descended en masse.

"I've got plenty of help, Papa. Why don't you and maman come the day after tomorrow. Bring Luc and his family with you. By then I'll be all settled. There are two people I want everyone to meet."

"Ah, oui?" The nuance in his father's tone meant Cesar had piqued his interest.

"Turn on the speaker so Maman can hear this, too." They were in for the shock of their lives.

Apparently Sarah had been more exhausted than even she'd realized because she never heard

Cesar come to bed. When Johnny came running in to the room the next morning to wake her up, Cesar was nowhere in sight. Only the indentation of his head on the pillow and the disappearance of the baby book gave proof that he'd spent the night next to her.

Had he been able to sleep?

She hoped so. He needed his strength to begin the uphill battle that would restore life to his legs. She chose to remember the doctor's prognosis in the most positive light.

"Guess what, Mommy?"

"Did you already have breakfast with your daddy?" It was after nine o'clock.

"Yes. Juliana made me cinnamon toast and juice."

His favorite. "That sounds good." She sat up and kissed the top of his head. He'd dressed in his blue plaid shorts and blue shirt with a T-rex on the front. "Where's your father now?"

"In the gym with his thair-pust."

"You mean therapist." Thank God. The doctor had warned her that every day he refused to get help, the faster his condition would deteriorate. This had to be the best sign!

Johnny nodded. "She speaks French with daddy."

She?

Sarah slid out of bed and drew on her pink robe. "What's her name?"

"Daddy calls her Bibi. Isn't that funny?"

"Very." Sarah made for the bathroom. She had a sinking feeling about this Bibi.

"She kind of looks like Tinker Bell."

Did she really?

Tinker Bell was the fetchingly shaped blond fairy who loved the fictional Peter Pan. A surprising stab of jealousy attacked her.

Over the years Sarah had struggled to keep the green eyed monster from ruining her life. Cesar had insisted he wouldn't marry until his career was over. She'd kept that uppermost in her mind every time the tabloids hinted at him being in another serious relationship.

"Daddy told Bianca to put her in the blue bedroom."

That comment, said from outside the door, caused her to drop the brush in the sink. "She's going to stay here?"

"Yup."

"For how long?" Sarah put on underwear before joining him. He followed her into the walk-in closet where she'd hung her things the night before.

"Bianca said for a long time."

Sarah felt the ground shake. She really was going to have to get her jealousy under control. The other woman was here to help Cesar. Sarah ought to be getting down on her knees to her.

"Hurry and get dressed, Mommy. Daddy said we're going to get me some toys."

"I remember."

If they were going to be walking around Positano, she'd better wear something appropriate as befitted Cesar's wife. There was little to choose from in the small wardrobe she'd brought. The sleeveless lightweight jersey dress with its all-over navy and white print would have to do.

When they were in town she'd shop for a few new outfits. Maybe they could drop off the throwaway camera at the same time to get their wedding pictures developed. Since her family hadn't been present at the ceremony, they'd want to see them.

She quickly slipped on the dress, pairing it

with navy sandals. As she emerged from the closet, she saw that Concetta had brought her a breakfast tray. Her breath caught to see cornflakes with bananas and strawberries. It was the same meal she and Cesar had eaten after making love all night.

He remembered… No one else knew how to twist the knife to heighten her pain to such exquisite proportions.

"While I eat, let's phone your grandparents."

"Can I tell them we live with daddy now?"

"You can tell them everything."

Together they sat down at the table. She dialed the house phone and handed it to him. Even if it was midnight in Carmel, she couldn't put it off any longer.

While she started to eat she heard, "Hi, Papa! Guess what?" In the next little while her son gave his grandparents an amazingly comprehensive description of everything that had gone on. He'd always been a happy boy, but there were degrees of happiness.

Being with his daddy had increased his capacity for joy. Already he was more complete, more confident. She could hear it in his voice.

Only a father who wanted his son as much as Cesar wanted him could have wrought this fantastic change in so short at time.

"Here, Mommy. They want to talk to you. I'm going to see if daddy's ready to go." With such an exciting day before him, naturally he couldn't sit still.

Sarah put the receiver to her ear with some trepidation. "Hi, you two. I'm sorry if we wakened you."

"You didn't. We've been lying here talking," her mother said. "Johnny's a new boy."

"I know."

"Now we can sleep." This from her father. "You've done the right thing, honey, even if we're going to miss you living so far away. What does the doctor say about Cesar's condition? We want the unvarnished truth."

Her hand tightened on the phone, fighting not to break down. "The nerves weren't severed. He is hopeful that with enough therapy Cesar will walk again. So am I."

"Oh, darling—" her mother cried for happiness.

"Don't count on it," came her husband's forbidding voice. He'd wheeled himself into the

bedroom so silently, she hadn't realized it. For once Johnny wasn't with him to announce their arrival. "Give me the phone, Sarah."

His forehead and eyebrows were beaded in perspiration. Whorls of damp black hair clung to the back of his neck. Large patches of sweat blotted his white T-shirt. Beneath his shorts, his hard-muscled legs glistened with moisture from his workout, the first since the accident. Judging by his grimace, it hadn't gone well. How could it have? This was only the beginning…

When she handed him the receiver, she knew he could feel her body trembling.

On his part he sounded comfortable talking with them. After all, he'd been a guest in their home many times. Despite everything that had happened, her father was in awe of Cesar and his accomplishments. But her husband made certain their conversation centered on Johnny.

"You'll have to fly over and visit us soon. I'll leave the arrangements to you and your daughter. Here she is."

Thrusting the receiver at her, he wheeled himself toward the bathroom. His mood was so grim, Sarah couldn't concentrate. She promised to call her parents back later, then hung up just as Angelo appeared. His arrival prevented any conversation. He nodded to her before following Cesar inside.

With a groan for what he had to face in order to facilitate his recovery, she picked up her purse and went in search of Johnny. His father needed privacy while he showered and dressed.

Since he wasn't on the main terrace, she went down another hallway until she heard voices. One of them was her son's, the other a woman who spoke English in heavily accented French. Sarah found them in the gym with its state-of-the-art equipment.

Though she'd love to scratch out the brown eyes of the attractive, toned blonde in her skimpy workout shorts and sports bra top, she knew it was a sentiment unworthy of her. *Bibi* was demonstrating the use of the barbells to a fascinated Johnny. Her ponytail swung back and forth.

"Mommy—look at me!"

It was impossible not to. "Great job!"

The other woman flashed her a smile. "Good morning, *signora*."

"How do you do, *signora,*" she said in kind.

"Everyone calls me Bibi."

"That's what I understand. I'm Sarah." They shook hands.

"One day your son will grow to be strong like his handsome papa."

"I'm sure of it." After a hesitation she said, "Bibi? How did it go this morning?"

She stood there with her hands on her hips. "He struggled, but that is to be expected. At least he came. In the hospital, he told me to get out."

Bibi had been there? "H-have you known him a long time?"

"Four years. I worked on his brother, and later a racing colleague of his."

"Who was that?"

"Arturo Scorzzi."

"I remember. He was almost killed."

"Yes, but now he is fully recovered. Cesar's doctor showed me his X-rays. In time your husband will be, too."

The information along with her positive declaration filled Sarah with fresh hope. Cesar wouldn't have hired her if she weren't the best therapist for his kind of injury.

"His problem is not just his body, Sarah. It is up here." She tapped her own temple. "He must visualize each movement before he tries to make one, but he is too impatient. In the beginning that is natural."

"How can I help?" she cried softly.

"When you're in bed at night, help him to turn on one side part of the night, then turn him on the other side later."

"What about his stomach?"

"Fine if that's what he wants. But when he's on his side, put the little pillow I gave him between his knees like this." Bibi demonstrated. She clearly thought Sarah and Cesar had a conjugal relationship.

"I can do that," Sarah said, having no wish to alter that assumption. "Anything else?"

"A good backrub will ease a lot of tension. Arms, hands, fingers, neck. It all helps. And make sure he comes to every session."

"We will," Johnny piped up. He'd put the bar bells down to listen.

"How often are they?"

"Four times a day for the present. After breakfast, after lunch, before dinner and before bed.

They are short in duration, but they will force the nerves to remember."

That was a strict regimen, but the other woman who looked to be Cesar's age knew what she was doing. No wonder she needed to live here. Sarah took back her unkind thoughts about Bibi.

"What will you do between sessions?"

She gestured with her hands. "I have a boyfriend. We do this and that when he's able to join me."

"I'm glad. And I'm thankful for you."

A look of speculation entered her eyes. "You are the new wife of the greatest racing champion alive. I think this is very hard on you."

Bibi understood a great deal.

"Johnny and I want him to walk again," she whispered tremulously.

"His sponsors and fans want the same thing. It is my job to make that happen. *Courage*," she said in French, reminding Sarah of the priest's words.

Courage was the operative word where Cesar was concerned. She nodded to Bibi, then grasped Johnny's hand. "Come on, honey." They left the gym.

"Daddy said to meet him at the car behind the pool."

“Do you need to use the bathroom or get a drink first?”

“Nope.”

“Okay. Let’s go.”

When they left the villa and walked through the portico, they discovered Angelo helping Cesar from the wheelchair into the back seat of a black luxury sedan.

He looked fabulous in a pair of tan chinos that covered his powerful thighs. Dressed in a navy-blue sport shirt revealing his broad shoulders and well-defined chest, the uninformed person wouldn’t know that a horrible injury afflicting the spine was hidden within his spectacular physique.

Johnny ran around the other side of the car so he could sit next to him. Sarah got in the front passenger side. After Angelo had stowed the wheelchair in the trunk, he took his place behind the wheel.

“Drive us to Fortuno’s, Angelo.”

“*Bene.*” The older man reversed the car to the road, then began the hairpin turns down to the town below. Flower scented air filled the interior. The dazzling sunlight bathing the villas and surrounding foliage almost blinded her.

“Is that a toy store, Daddy?”

"A big one. When I'm home I always get your cousins' presents there. Have you decided what you want to buy?" Cesar asked his son.

"Mommy wrote it down for me cos I don't write very good yet."

"You don't write very *well,*" she corrected him.

"Let's have a look, Sarah."

It was the first time since yesterday evening that he'd spoken to her directly. She opened her purse and took out the list. Whenever she was around Cesar, her hands seemed to be permanently unsteady. When she turned to give the paper to him, their fingers brushed, fanning her fire.

Their eyes met as if he'd felt her heat and was scorched by it. Though the moment was only a fraction in time, she thought maybe he was remembering the way it used to be between them. But in a flash he pulled out his sunglasses and put them on, shutting her out more effectively than an eclipse of the sun.

She faced straight ahead again. It took time to negotiate the heavy traffic before Angelo pulled away from the stream of cars into an alley behind the store in question. He came to a stop next to a truck and got out the wheelchair.

While Johnny steadied it, the older man assisted Cesar from the car without problem. "I'll wait here for you."

"*Grazie,* Angelo."

The older man rang the buzzer at the side of the rear doors, then got back in the vehicle. Evidently Cesar had made prior arrangements with the management. Such heavy crowds out on Positano's main streets would have made it impossible for Angelo to find parking.

Johnny smiled at them while they waited for someone to answer. "Hey—we all look alike!" He spoke the truth. One way or another their clothes matched. Everyone in blue.

Cesar and son had come to town.

The moment the back door opened, their lives were no longer their own. Word had spread that the famous Cesar Villon, Positano's favorite son, was on the premises. After wheeling himself inside, he was besieged by staff and customers alike wanting to shake hands and get autographs. It was impossible to do any shopping.

Tourists with cameras or cell phones took pictures of the three of them. Customers buying merchandise with his name on the packaging begged him to sign their purchases. Shouts in every language including English told him they were praying for him. His heart couldn't help but be warmed by the deep affection demonstrated.

For Sarah, it was a joy to see how much people cared. But Johnny on the other hand pressed against Cesar's legs, utterly bewildered by the near mob scene. Cesar noticed it immediately.

"I shouldn't have brought you in here," he muttered, squeezing Johnny's hand. Normally he handled the masses with calm and finesse, but this situation was different. He'd brought his son to do something special for him like any father. His frustration level had to be off the charts.

Sarah had been around screaming out-of-control fans at the racetrack for most of her life, especially when Cesar flew in for the big race. But this was Johnny's first experience with his father out in public. It was something he would never like, but would have to get used to. Now was the time to teach him his first lesson in dealing with his father's fame.

She looked at her son clinging to Cesar. "Don't be nervous, honey. This always happens when people see your daddy. That's why the security and police have arrived. They've posted themselves throughout the store to keep people away so you and your daddy can find the toys you want to take home. Ignore them.

"I'll push the cart along while you two get started. The racetrack games are down this aisle. This is going to fun!"

The anxious expression on his face turned into a smile. "Come on, Daddy."

With the crisis averted, they spent the next hour picking out the same kinds of toys he had at home but couldn't bring, plus some new ones. Enough to fill three shopping carts by the time they'd finished.

In excellent English the manager of the store asked Johnny if he wanted anything else. The clerk was ringing up the bill.

"Do you have any sunglasses like my daddy's?"

"I will find out." The other man snapped his fingers and called to another clerk in rapid Italian. Almost instantly a pair was produced.

Johnny put them on and turned to his father, oblivious to the fascinated audience hanging out in the store to watch from a distance. "Now we both look cool!"

Only recently had Johnny picked up that word from one of his friends who had an older brother. She heard Cesar chuckle. "You look very cool, *piccolo mio*." They high-fived each other.

People started clapping. Out of the corner of her eye Sarah saw that several photojournalists had entered the store and were getting everything on tape for the evening news.

One of them shouted something in Italian to Cesar. Without turning to the man, Cesar called back in English, "If you want an interview, speak to my wife. She's my publicist now. Come on, Johnny," he whispered out of earshot. "Let's take our things to the car."

As they left the counter, the media converged on her like a swarm of bees. "*Per favore,* Signora de Falcon, when did you first meet Cesar? What's your name? What's your son's name? How long have you been married? Did you see the crash?" The questions came fast and furiously.

Cesar had dropped this squarely in her lap, hoping to embarrass her. Payback time for the way she'd exploded her bomb in front of him at the hospital.

By tonight the whole world was going to know

everything anyway, so she decided to be as truthful as possible without getting into areas that were no one's business but theirs. Taking on a calm profile, she smiled into the video cams.

"As you can see, my husband's occupied at the moment. I'm Sarah Priestley de Falcon. We met when he came to race at the U.S. Grand Prix in Monterey, California, nine years ago. My father, Edward Priestley, owns the track. After Cesar's spectacular world championship win, my parents hosted a party for him at our home. I was only seventeen at the time. It was love at first sight for me."

Her voice caught. "I discovered that it's a great responsibility to be in love with anyone who has such a rare talent. He's been gifted like few others in the history of racing. All this time I've had to share him with his fans. So has our son, Jean-Cesar, who came along five years ago.

"While Cesar's getting back on his feet to race in the first Grand Prix of the season at Monza next year, the three of us are going to spend some quality time together."

"Then he's not permanently injured?"

"You mean you believe the fairy tale your colleagues have been spreading?" But she smiled as she said it. "Can you actually imagine anything keeping the great Cesar Villon down? If you can, then your imagination is better than mine. He's already working out four times a day and will be back better than ever in no time. That's a heads-up for his competitors by the way.

"Now if you'll excuse us, our son is waiting for his daddy to put his new racetrack together at home." As she started for the rear of the store, there was a huge roar and a cheer from the crowd. People had come in from the streets.

The chants of "Cesar! Cesar! Cesar!" echoed until she exited the rear door.

When she reached the car, Angelo helped her inside. The two in the back seat were poring over Johnny's new PalmPilot. Cesar was showing him how it worked.

"Look, Mommy—" He put his hand over her shoulder so she could see. He'd used the metal stylus to print his name in his own irregular style. Big letters that couldn't fit on one line, all lower case.

j o h n

n y

p f a l c

on.

"That's fantastic!"

"I know."

Spontaneous laughter rumbled out of Cesar. A sound of delight that started in the belly. Yesterday morning she couldn't have imagined hearing anything close to it.

Much as she wanted to do some other shopping, now wasn't the time. The hordes of people pouring into Positano made it almost impossible for Angelo to maneuver at the noon hour. Tomorrow would be soon enough. While Cesar worked out, Sarah would take a walk into town with Johnny.

At the moment, their son couldn't wait to get home and start playing with all his new toys. Being with his father was like having all his Christmases rolled into one.

As for Cesar, she imagined this outing had exhausted him emotionally. To face people after his injury took a tremendous amount of courage. But she had the satisfaction of knowing he'd made it through this morning's ordeal. With this hurdle overcome, it would be a little easier to face the next one.

Clearly he was willing to do anything for Johnny's sake. Just as she'd suspected, their son played *the* crucial role in his father's progress. She would milk it for all it was worth to get him walking again.

Once they'd returned to the villa, everyone including the maids helped take the packages inside. While Sarah freshened up in the bathroom, she soon heard cries and whoops of laughter coming from Johnny's bedroom. When she went to investigate she discovered Cesar had already assembled the new racetrack set on the table. With the giant packs of batteries purchased, they'd be able to play indefinitely.

Johnny was in ecstasy. Who wouldn't be with a father who knew more about racing than anyone alive? She noticed everything else was still waiting to be opened and put away.

Sarah looked for the new bedding they'd bought. She pulled everything from the wrappers and started to make up her son's bed. Tonight he would sleep on sheets and pillows covered in his adored dinosaurs. As she was throwing the dinosaur comforter over the bed, Bianca came in to announce that lunch was ready on the terrace.

Several hours later, while Johnny and his father were swimming in the pool with Angelo and Bibi, Sarah put a superheroes lamp on his bedside table. A poster of the latest comic book hero movie adorned the wall above his bed. Those were the last finishing touches. The bedroom had been transformed and now resembled his room in Watsonville stuffed full with the treasures that made it home for him.

Anyone peeking inside would know a little boy lived here. Cesar's little boy.

Along with a soccer ball and a shiny red Italian scooter he could ride around the gym, his father had bought him some fairy tales published in Italian, French and Spanish.

Sarah had a feeling formal language lessons were about to begin with Cesar the teacher—required education for a Varano-de Falcon. She wasn't complaining. Sarah would need those lessons, too, the sooner the better.

When Bianca spoke Italian in Sarah's presence, she felt shut out. Cesar seemed to understand this because he stressed to the entire staff including Bibi that everyone speak English in front of Sarah and Johnny until they were acclimatized.

Though she knew Cesar would always despise her, she appreciated his sensitivity.

By the end of their busy day she was worn-out. While Cesar disappeared for his final workout session with Bibi, Sarah put Johnny down, then took a long bath herself.

But unlike the night before, she was still awake when Cesar wheeled in to their bedroom for his shower. Though she pretended to be asleep while Angelo helped him into bed, her body quickened to know he lay so close to her.

He'd brought the familiar smell of his soap with him. Combined with his male scent, her senses were instantly aroused. She crushed the edge of the pillow in her hands.

Even in the semidark Cesar must have seen the betraying gesture. "Sarah?"

Her heart began to thud. "Yes?"

CHAPTER SIX

"TURN around so I can talk to you."

For a moment Sarah had forgotten that Cesar had to lie on his back and couldn't move the bottom half of his body.

She rolled to her other side so she was facing him. Above the covers she could see his bare arms and chest with its dusting of hair. Her insides quivered in remembrance of the night they'd spent giving each other pleasure beyond comprehension.

"My family's coming tomorrow to stay through the weekend. They'll be arriving some time in the later afternoon."

Sarah had known it was going to happen, but she was frightened. "Do you wish they weren't coming this soon?"

"It's out of my hands." Over and above his frustration, he sounded resigned.

"Like any mother, she needs to see you with her own eyes and discover that her son is well on the road to a full recovery."

"What she sees is what it's going to be from here on," he bit out. "It's Johnny that has her sounding happier than I've heard her in years. She would have come tonight if I'd given the word."

"He can't wait to meet his other grandparents." She bit her lip. "As they're *your* parents, I know they'll treat me with every courtesy, but I have no illusions about their innermost feelings where I'm concerned."

He lay there with one hard-muscled arm over his eyes. "At the moment they're too overjoyed to realize they're grandparents again to think about anything else."

It was a lot more than that. Fearing that Cesar would never be able to father a child period, this news had to mean everything to them. A child brought new life. Johnny had brought Cesar back from the edge. They knew he was the reason their son had left the hospital this fast, the reason he had started his therapy.

"W-what can I do to help?"

"You?" His voice mocked. "Nothing."

His curt response cut her to the quick. "Would you rather I made myself scarce while they're here?"

"Johnny wouldn't tolerate it."

"Of course he would."

"Lie to anyone but me. You're his mother. He knows where you are every second of the day and night, and if he doesn't, he goes to find you. That kind of bond takes years to develop."

Unshed tears stung her eyelids. "He has loved you since I showed him your picture from the first months of his life. From the beginning not a day has gone by that he hasn't brought up your name, wanting to know where you are, what race you're getting ready for. He goes to sleep with his daddy's name on lips.

"When you picked him up from your hospital bed, he launched himself into your arms with all the love he has in him. In case you've forgotten, when it grew tense in the store today he clung to *you*, not me. I'd be jealous if it were anyone but you."

A deep sigh escaped his throat. "Was it a normal delivery, or did you have complications?"

She couldn't keep up with his thoughts. "No

complications. But there was a small time period right after the baby was born when I couldn't feel anything from my waist down because of the epidural. I had some anxious moments until it started to wear off.

"It's probably the closest I'll ever come to knowing something of what it's like for you," she whispered in pain.

His arm shifted back to the mattress. "How long were you in labor?"

"About thirty hours."

He stirred. "That long?"

"It's normal for a first baby."

"What about Johnny?"

"He was perfect in every way."

"Did you nurse him?"

"Yes."

"For how long?"

"Until he was nine months."

Trying to reassure him she said, "You can trust the pictures in his baby book. Our son has been a gift from day one."

She could hear his mind turning everything over. "His two-year-old photo looks like one of Luc at the same age."

"Your mother will probably tell you all the rest look like you."

After an uneasy silence he said, "My brother and Olivia will be coming with my parents. They're bringing Marie-Claire."

The news relieved her somewhat. "How fun for Johnny. He's very good around Lacey, Elaine's little girl. She adores her older cousin of course, and follows him everywhere. He pretends not to like it, but I know he *loves* being idolized." He's got all your charisma, Cesar.

"While he was brushing his teeth tonight, one of his bottom teeth came out in the front. It disappeared down the drain before I could catch it."

Sarah laughed gently. "I'm glad you were there. He hates blood."

"I noticed."

"I didn't hear him cry for me, Cesar."

Silence reigned before he said, "No."

"And you know why. Because he was with his daddy. That was all he needed. As long as we're on the subject of his fears, you should know that if he ever freezes on you for no apparent reason, it's because there's a fly somewhere around. He hates them. I made a mistake when I let him watch an animated film about flies. He wasn't ready for it."

It was Cesar's turn to chuckle. Always a beautiful sound she couldn't hear often enough.

"Cesar?" She raised up on her elbow, wanting to take advantage of this lull when he didn't seem so hostile. "Bibi told me you need to be moved to different positions during the night. I'd go crazy if I had to stay in the same position all the time. Why don't you let me turn you toward me now?"

"Angelo will come." His steely voice felt like a sudden blast of arctic air.

"There's no need with me right here."

She felt his anger. "There's every need."

Anger masked fear. It gave her an idea.

"What are you afraid of?"

"What in the hell are you talking about?"

"Whether you're wearing pajama bottoms or not, I've seen your body before. We made a baby together. It's no mystery to me." After the incredible night they'd spent together, he ought to know that.

"The doctor told me there's not a scratch on you. The injury's deep inside, so what difference does it make to you if I spare Angelo from having to get up in the night? Unless of course my touch is so repulsive to you, you can't bear the thought of my hands on your body. Then I understand and won't offend you again by offering."

The silence grew louder. "It's been a long day. Go to sleep, Sarah."

Before she turned away from him she said, "If you should change your mind, just whisper to me and I'll help you."

Half an hour later Sarah was still wide-awake. So was Cesar. His restlessness indicated growing discomfort.

This had gone on long enough. "When will Angelo be here?"

He didn't pretend to be out for the count. "At two, and again at four."

Her watch said midnight. "Neither of us can wait that long."

Whether she had his permission or not, she threw off the covers, revealing Cesar's long, powerful, pajama-clad legs to her vision. He was built like a Roman god.

Trying to focus on the task at hand, she got on her knees and reached across him. His warmth rose up to engulf her. With both hands on his left hip she carefully started to roll him toward her. It didn't seem possible he couldn't do it himself.

Their bodies brushed against each other in the process. He perforce had to adjust his head and arms to the new position.

"There! That *has* to feel better."

"It does," he admitted with telling reluctance.

"Good!"

She fit the small pillow lying at the end of the bed between his knees the way Bibi had shown her.

"In a little while I'll help you turn on your stomach. I know it's the way you prefer to sleep." The comment slipped out before she could stop it, but it was too late to call it back now.

Many were the times in the past when they'd lounged on the beach at Carmel. Sometimes after a race he would fall asleep from exhaustion and she would watch him. Inevitably he would turn on his stomach with his arms stretched beyond his dark head. A gorgeous specimen of manhood she longed to keep captive on her shore while she stood guard over him.

Would that she were one of those Sirens with the magic power to drive him mad with desire once more.

"Tonight when Angelo comes, tell him you won't need him anymore. I'm not only your new publicist. As of now I'm Bibi's new assistant."

So saying, she got out of bed and padded into the bathroom for her lotion. Feeling enabled since he'd told her he was more comfortable in the changed position, she intended to help make him even more relaxed.

After returning to the side of the bed, she poured some of it onto his left shoulder. Then she sat down next to him and began smoothing it into his beautiful, smooth olive skin stretched over hard muscle. She worked slowly, covering every centimeter of exposed flesh from his neck and back, down his arm to his left hand. A hand that had been gripping the steering wheel of various Formula 1 race cars since he was nineteen years old.

With another dollop of lotion she massaged his palm, finding the places in between his strong, ringless fingers. She loved the contrast of calluses only to find those tiny areas of soft skin. On her next trip to town she planned to buy him a wedding band. A simple one in gold. Whether he chose to wear it or not was immaterial. Inside the band she would have it engraved with a private message.

After keeping Johnny a secret from him for so long, he could accuse her all he wanted of not knowing the meaning of love. But he couldn't deny what had happened between them the night Johnny had been conceived. Theirs had been a union of fire. She still burned from the memories and craved to know his possession again.

It took the greatest strength of will not to put her lips to the skin she'd been touching and kneading. The urge to find his mouth with her own and make love to him for hour upon hour was fast becoming an obsession. If he was incapable of making love to her the old-fashioned way, none of that mattered. He was the love of her life. She would show him. Nothing was impossible.

Finally she heard the sounds of deep breathing and knew he'd drifted off. After four grueling workouts on top of everything else today, it didn't surprise her. She put the lotion on the bedside table and pulled the covers to his neck.

"Sleep well, my love," she mouthed the words. On impulse she tiptoed to Johnny's room and peeked inside. All was well. With both her men safely tucked in for the night, she could settle down. But there didn't seem to be any way to shut off her mind.

Tomorrow she'd be meeting Cesar's family. Another trial of fire.

Courage, the priest had said. Where did one go to find it?

"*Eh bien,* Bibi—looking as beautiful as ever I see. Haven't you finished torturing him yet?"

"*Tiens tiens!* If it isn't Luca de Falcon. The terrible two in one room," she teased.

From the exercise table Cesar eyed his tall, dark-haired elder brother who'd just walked in the gym. He looked good. "Bibi invented the word," he said on a groan.

Luc grinned. "Tell me about it. I've been where you are, little brother."

Once upon a time there had been a question whether Luc would keep his right leg, let alone ever be able to use it again. Bad news for a world-class alpine skier. Though he couldn't ski anymore, Bibi had been one of the therapists to help him walk again. A few years ago he'd been able to throw away his cane, the lucky devil.

"Five more knee-ups, then he's all yours, *mon vieux.*"

"You're all heart, Bibi," Luc muttered. "In that case I'd better do something ahead of time to counteract the effect of Juliana's cooking or Olivia will divorce me." He picked up a set of barbells and got started.

"Since when?" Cesar asked through gritted teeth. Bibi gave no quarter.

"Since I got on the scales last week and discovered I'm ten pounds heavier than a year ago."

"Your wife is right to get after you." Bibi entered into the conversation. "She wants you around for a long time."

Finally she gave a friendly pat to Cesar's shoulder. "You're done until tonight." She helped him from the exercise table to the wheelchair. "Now I'm off for a swim. *À toute à l'heure.*"

Cesar wheeled after her. Once she was out of the door, he locked it. When he turned around, Luc was right behind him. He glimpsed the compassion in his brother's eyes before he felt his arms go around him. They hugged while silent messages passed between them. But when he finally let Cesar go, those silver orbs similar to his own were dancing.

"You're so full of surprises, I still haven't recovered."

Cesar drew in a fortifying breath. "I'm afraid Sarah was the one with the surprise."

"She's *ravissante, mon frère*. You know what I mean," he said in a deep voice meant for no one else's ears but his.

Yes. Cesar knew. Last night his Siren had treated him to a new dimension of the word torture.

"Those eyes—it's no longer a mystery why there was a time when you found California more enticing than the usual grazing grounds closer to home. As for Johnny, I'm completely *bouleversé*."

"So am I."

"After we were introduced, the first thing he did was show me where he'd lost a tooth. He then informed me that *you* weren't scared of anything, not even blood. That's high praise for a son to give his father." Laughter poured out of Luc.

Cesar laughed with him till the tears came. "He's so wonderful I can't find the words."

Luc nodded. "He has Maman enchanted. She can't stop crying. Marie-Claire is already his slave. But you should see Papa! He hasn't let go of Jean-Cesar's hand. At the moment your son is taking his *grand-père* on a tour of your house. Already he's playing the host. He's a Falcon all right."

They stared hard at each other. "He's one of us," Cesar whispered. "Incredible, isn't it?"

Luc cocked his head. "You couldn't have chosen a name to make papa prouder."

Cesar looked away from his brother. "That was Sarah's doing. She put it on the birth certificate five years ago."

"She's done a remarkable job of raising your son. You certainly met your equal in Carmel. She has all the right instincts." And all the right parts in all the right places. That's what he knew Luc wanted to say, but to his credit he didn't.

"Except for one fatal flaw. I don't want to talk about her."

"Then we won't."

Luc reached out to unlock the door. "Let's get you back to your room before Bianca bites our heads off that we're ruining Juliana's dinner."

"Johnny already has her wrapped around his little finger."

"Like father, like son. She always liked you better than me." Luc's eyebrows lifted. "Did I ever tell you I was jealous about that?"

"Did I ever tell you how jealous I was of my famous ski champion brother?"

"Those days are over for me. Let's thank God you'll recover in time to race again next year."

Cesar stiffened. *"Et tu, brute?"*

Luc shrugged his shoulders. "I'm only repeating your wife's words in front of the camera yesterday. Olivia and I happened to see her on last night's news."

A band constricted his breathing. He'd purposely not watched. "What exactly did she say?"

Luc gave him a verbatim report. "She was magnificent. To save face you *have* to get better now."

Cesar's gracious parents and brother shocked Sarah by hugging her the moment he made the introductions. She saw no censure in their eyes as they welcomed her to the family. Any strong feelings against her were lost in the joy they felt because Cesar had survived the crash and was looking so well already.

And of course, there was Johnny who took their hearts by storm. "Oh Cesario—he looks just like you at the same age!" his mother cried.

"Come here and let me hug you again, Giovanni. You don't mind if I call you that,do you?"

The name Giovanni triggered something Sarah had said to Cesar in the hospital because he shot her a brief, narrow-lidded glance.

"I like it!" Johnny's comment caused everyone to laugh in delight. Like all Cesar's family, he had their charm.

Later that night Olivia leaned toward Sarah. "While everyone's still out on the terrace with the children, there's something I want to give you in private before we all go to bed. Come with me."

Intrigued, Sarah followed her sister-in-law through the house to the guest bedroom prepared for them. Olivia was one of the famous blond Duchess triplets from New York. The other two were married to Cesar's cousins.

Sarah found her warm and down to earth. After supervising their children throughout dinner and afterward, they'd already become good friends.

Once the door was closed, Olivia darted to the closet. "I put it in here." Sarah assumed it was a wedding present, or something for Johnny. To her surprise she produced a cane of all things. She hurried back to Sarah with it.

"You heard Cesar's parents talking about Luc's injury tonight, but you don't know the history behind this cane. When I first met Luc, he'd barely started using it to get around. He was in so much pain physically and emotionally, it was awful to witness.

"Seeing Cesar in that wheelchair tonight was like déjà vu. They're very much alike and so close. But there was a time when Luc thought Cesar had betrayed him with his fiancée."

Sarah stared at the floor. "I read about the scandal in the paper."

"None of it was true, Sarah. She'd had a secret affair with one of Cesar's mechanics and tried to pass off the baby as Cesar's whom she believed had more money than Luc because of his fame. What she did was evil. It almost destroyed both brothers because Luc believed her lies."

"I wish I'd known!" Sarah cried. "It's the reason I kept putting off calling Cesar. I thought—" She buried her face in her hands. "I thought if he already had a baby, he didn't need to hear about another one. How awful for them, for the whole family."

A groan came out of Olivia. "You have no idea

how ugly things got, especially when Cesar had been going through a long, ongoing personal crisis of his own he wouldn't share with anyone. I think maybe you had something to do with that, Sarah."

"If I did," she said, lifting her head, "I was the last person to know it. Tell me everything."

"Luc refused to speak to Cesar who was totally innocent. To make matters worse, I went to watch Cesar race at Monza. Through a horrible misunderstanding, Luc thought I'd slept with him and wanted nothing to do with me. If you could have heard the things he said to me…"

Tears rolled down Sarah's cheeks. "Then you should have been in Cesar's hospital room the other morning when he found out he had a son I'd never told him about…"

Olivia put a comforting arm around her for a moment. "They're not brothers for nothing."

"No." Sarah sniffed, trying to gain her composure.

"Because of what happened with Luc's fiancée, Cesar has great reason to distrust any woman who tries to get close to him."

"He despises me, Olivia."

"He only thinks he does."

Sarah shook her head. "I did such a horrible thing to him, Olivia, there's no way I can expect his forgiveness. If only I could go back and rectify things." She sobbed. "When I see how much Johnny loves the family, how much he's needed all of you and his father, it kills me. I'm an evil person."

"No—" Olivia cried.

"Oh, yes, I am. After what I did to Cesar, it's a wonder he didn't sue for full custody of Johnny." Her voice shook. "He had every right to take him away from me."

"He would never do that to the mother of his son. He's a remarkable man."

"I know," Sarah whispered.

"Once I'd heard the truth from Cesar about Luc's fiancée, I went back to the sailboat to talk to Luc about it. I told him what Cesar had related to me. At the time, he wouldn't believe me. The next thing I knew, he'd left for Monaco.

"All that remained behind was a cruel note to me. I found the cane on the floor. It meant Luc could finally walk without help. It also meant he didn't want anything to do with me ever again.

"It was a nightmare because I loved him so much. Unable to get through to him, I went back to New York and took the cane with me. But there was a happy ending. Luc found the courage to face Cesar and they reconciled. Now they're closer than ever, and obviously Luc and I got together."

Olivia looked at the cane. "To me it represents the bridge between Luc's darkest hell and his journey back into the light.

"When I saw you on the news last night and heard your conviction that Cesar would be back next year to win another race, I knew you had to have the cane because in time I, too, believe he'll walk again. When he reaches a certain point, he'll need it for a while. Let it be your good luck talisman."

"What a priceless gift." Sarah reached out to hug her. "I'll hide it until the right moment." Cesar was in no state of mind to handle seeing it yet. "Thank you for telling me what I needed to know, Olivia. It helps me understand Cesar in ways I never could have done without your explanation."

"You're welcome. Let's be honest. We're married to the most fantastic men alive, but until every possible obstacle has been obliterated from their paths, they guard their hearts fiercely."

That's what the priest had said. He'd also promised that one day the sun would come out. Olivia had said much the same thing. Sarah gripped the cane tighter as a little frisson of hope chased up her spine.

"Excuse me for a minute while I find a place for it, then I'll join you and the others." She knew exactly where she would put it and headed for Johnny's room.

Once her mission was accomplished, she followed the noise of happy laughter back to the terrace. Earlier Johnny had brought out his game of twister. While the adults watched, he did amazing contortions.

Marie-Claire, with blond curls bobbing against her forehead, tried to imitate him and fell flat several times. Trying not to laugh too hard, Luc helped her get up and attempted to repair his daughter's wounded pride with words of encouragement.

Cesar on the other hand secretly aided and abetted his son from the wheelchair. The friendly spirit of competition between brothers would always be there, but Marie-Claire had worn herself out.

Olivia darted Sarah an amused glance before she said, "I think it's bathtime."

"Hey—she can swim in Mommy and Daddy's tub with me!"

Johnny's comment caused the family to roar with laughter. Cesar caught his son to him and pulled him onto his lap. "That's what the swimming pool is for. You can swim with her tomorrow. Right now it's time for bed."

"Okay," Johnny said with a long face.

Before she could say it, Cesar prompted his son to kiss everyone good-night. He jumped off his father's lap and did his bidding before leaving the terrace with him. Again, this was a proud moment for her husband, one in which Sarah didn't want to interfere.

Cesar's parents had decided to retire, too. While everyone said good-night, she gathered up the game and followed behind Luc who was carrying an overly tired, overwrought Marie-Claire in his arms.

While Cesar supervised Johnny's bath, Sarah straightened his bedroom, which looked like a disaster. Then she slipped into the other room to grant them their quiet time. Eventually he came running in to give her a toothpaste kiss, then hurried back to his daddy.

It was almost eleven before Angelo helped Cesar to bed. Though she was exploding with thoughts and feelings she'd been storing all day, she was too afraid of being rebuffed to initiate conversation. But as soon as they were alone, she turned to him only to discover him lying on his left side away from her.

"Cesar? Did you tell Angelo I'll help you in the night from now on?"

Though they weren't touching, she could feel the tremor that shook his body. "I told him to come at four."

Her pulse picked up speed. "Then I'll set my watch for two."

"If you sleep through it, don't worry about it."

"I won't." She bit her lower lip. "I—I like your family very much."

"Where did you and Olivia disappear to for so long?"

She moaned inwardly. Sarah had been waiting for that question, but he'd asked it without acknowledging what she'd just said. If she was hoping that seeing his family had done anything to ameliorate the tension between them, she could think again.

"Olivia didn't know how much I knew about Luc's accident."

"His wasn't anything like mine. Even if he'd lost his leg, he had another one."

"I know. Basically s-she told me not to give up hope." Olivia had told her a lot of things that Cesar didn't need to hear.

He cursed softly. "The platitudes never end."

That made her angry and she sat up. "Would you prefer that everyone tell you it's hopeless? How would you like it if your family simply shook their heads and said, "You poor thing. You're all washed up. You should have died out there." Her body was shaking uncontrollably.

"It's what they're all thinking," his voice grated.

"No, Cesar—that's what *you're* thinking. It's pathetic!"

She threw her covers aside and jumped out of bed.

"Where in the hell are you going?"

Well, well. She'd made him fighting mad. That

was good. Would that he'd get so outraged, he'd leap out of bed to come and strangle her.

"Away from you so you can wallow in self-pity. It's what you want. I'll sleep with Johnny for the rest of the night. Thankfully he has no idea the father he worships has given up." At the doorway she turned to him. "Don't worry. I'll be back at two."

CHAPTER SEVEN

THE night was endless.

Every time Cesar glanced at his watch, only five minutes had passed.

Since Sarah had swept out of the bedroom in a rage, memories of that day at the track had started coming back to him in flashes. The details weren't clear yet, but he relived that feeling he was careering to his death again and again. His body broke out in a cold sweat.

Whether he closed his eyes or kept them open, the horror of it left him gasping for breath.

"Cesar?"

He smelled Sarah's fragrance before she sat down next to him. Part of her flowing, lilac colored nightgown brushed against his arm. "What's wrong? I heard you cry out."

"It's nothing."

"Don't tell me that." She put a hand to his cheek.

He felt her fingers brush the hair off his forehead. “You’re hot, and you’ve been perspiring.” She moved away. In seconds she came back with a cold, damp washrag and wiped his face with it.

“You’ve remembered the crash, haven’t you. The doctor told me your mind would recall the moment of impact when it was ready. It means you’re healing.”

He groaned. If this was healing, he didn’t want any part of it.

“I saw the whole thing. Is there anything you want to ask me?”

Cesar felt his eyelids sting. “How did Johnny handle it?”

She moved the cloth down the side of his jaw to his throat, giving him more relief. “Ever since the first time he saw you walk to your race car, he assumed you wore an astronaut suit. It’s a good thing he considers them indestructible. When you crashed he said, “He won’t die cos he’s wearing his astronaut suit, Mommy.”

The blood pounded in his ears. “What did you say to that?”

“I told him, ‘That’s right. The great Cesar Villon is indestructible.’”

He inhaled harshly. "Is that what *you* thought?"

She stared down at him in the semidarkness. "No. Unfortunately I'm too grown up to believe in fairy tales. I just kept praying to God to preserve your life so you could meet your son and love him the way I do."

"It appears your prayer was answered."

"But not yours, right Cesar?"

Her salvo went straight to his gut. "I'll refresh the washrag. Then I'll be back to help you get in a different position."

He waited in agony for her return. In truth, he didn't want to be alone tonight….

"Which way do you want to lie next?" She'd put the cloth on the bedside table.

"On my back."

"Okay." She removed the covers. He was dressed in fresh pajama bottoms. "When I say three, you start to turn and I'll do the rest."

She put her hands beneath his hip and knees. "Ready? One, two, three—" Over he went on his back. She was strong when she had to be. As Luc had pointed out, Sarah Priestley had many attributes.

After putting the little pillow at the end of the

bed, she made sure his legs were straight. "Does that feel better?"

"Yes."

Once she'd pulled up the covers to his waist, she sat down and began to wipe his bare chest and shoulders with the damp cloth. "Tell me when to stop."

Damn if he didn't want her to stop. "When I saw Johnny and Marie-Claire playing together, I realized how much he needs friends his own age. We need to get him into school right away."

"I was going to talk to you about that, Cesar. His kindergarten class in Watsonville started last week."

"We start a little later here. The family will be leaving Sunday evening. I'll inquire about it on Monday. He's going to have to be mainstreamed."

She nodded. "It's the best way."

"You agree?" He was relieved they wouldn't have an argument about that. Johnny wouldn't like it at first.

"When I was in grade school, the kids who came from other countries were tossed in at the deep end. Within a year they were spouting English as if they'd lived there all their lives.

Children always pick everything up so fast. By this time next year we won't know Johnny from any of the other children here."

Exactly. "Except that with English his native language, he'll have an advantage."

"Yes. The best of you and me," she said in a raw tone, catching him off guard.

"Next summer we'll stay at the house in Monaco. Marie-Claire will be a year older."

"After a year of Italian, his French will come fast." She had read his mind. "Do you have a headache? Your ibuprofen is in the bathroom. If nothing else it might help you sleep now."

If he needed oblivion, it was to shut her from his thoughts for the rest of the night. In the face of her ministrations, it was impossible to maintain the same level of anger.

"Bring me four."

"Please," she corrected him the way she did Johnny. "Along with your desire to give up, you appear to have lost your manners, too. Being paralyzed is no excuse," came the sharp retort.

Cesar had no idea he'd married a woman with a biting tongue. The girl he'd made love to didn't have a mean bone in her beautiful body. But he had to admit that in six years that body was more alluring than ever. He also had to admit she was a perfect mother to their son. Cesar's mother had sung her new daughter-in-law's praises to him more than once since their arrival.

"*Per favore*, Signora de Falcon."

"That's better."

On that crisp note she withdrew the cloth and left him long enough to bring back his pills with a glass of water. After he'd swallowed them she started toward Johnny's door.

"If I ask you politely this time, will you read me a story so I can go to sleep?"

She swung around in surprise. Her nightgown swirled around her long, gorgeous legs. "What story?"

"Sleeping Beauty." Except that it was like he'd been the one asleep all the years they'd been apart and was just now coming awake. "It's in Johnny's room on his desk."

"It's in Italian!"

"I'll help you."

"In other words you're ready to start *my* lessons *now*. I guess it won't hurt to become proficient so I can understand my son when he curses in both languages like his father."

"Is that what I do?" he mocked.

"In four languages actually, depending on your mood. As you know, I'm awfully good at slaughtering Italian. But if you really want me to, it's your funeral."

"I'll chance it since it'll get my mind off the one I escaped in Brazil."

Her face closed up. "That's not funny, Cesar."

"It wasn't meant to be."

Before long she was back with the illustrated book in question. She turned on the lamp on her side of the bed and got in under the covers. Though she moved fast, it wasn't quite fast enough to hide the feminine contours of her silk-clad figure from his gaze.

In that instant he felt a stunning physical response of desire for her. Not just in his mind. *It affected every centimeter of his body, inside and out!*

Dear God— He'd thought he was dead in that part of his anatomy. Did that mean—

"Cesar? Your breathing sounds ragged all of sudden. Are you ill? Tell me the truth!"

His heart thundered in his chest. He needed to

talk to his doctor as soon as possible. "I guess I'm still reliving the crash," he lied to give himself time to comprehend what was happening.

"Then let's get my lesson started." She opened the cover to the first page. *"La Bella Addormentata,"* she began, trying her hardest to pronounce the words so he'd understand them.

In one night he'd been in bed with two women, but it was his sweet, loving Sarah from that other life who lay next to him right now. Despite the terrible thing she'd done to him, his passion for her was back, stronger than ever.

It took all his strength of will not to reach out and pull her on top of his body. The need to feel her against him, to taste her mouth was such exquisite torture he groaned.

"Cesar—" she cried.

"Keep reading," he demanded. "Please…"

"Johnny, honey? Everyone's ready to leave." It was four in the afternoon. Cesar's family had a plane to catch.

He looked up at Sarah with a sad face. "Do they have to go?" That look brought searing guilt to the surface. For five years she'd deprived him of this.

"I'm afraid so, but you heard your father. We'll visit them next month."

Olivia walked over to them carrying her daughter who was inconsolable at having to leave. "Johnny? Do you know where Albert went? Marie-Claire can't find him. He's that little lamb that goes with her set of farm animals."

He lifted his eyebrows. "I don't know. She was playing with them everywhere."

"Maybe it's in your bedroom," Cesar suggested. "Let's take a look."

"I'll help, too," Sarah murmured. She eyed Olivia. "We'll be right back. If we can't find it, we'll keep looking and send it to you. There won't be any peace until she gets it back."

"You're right," Olivia said, sounding harried.

Sarah and Johnny hurried after Cesar who wheeled down the hall with greater energy than usual. Since Friday night when he'd had a breakthrough of memory, he seemed different. He wasn't quite so hostile with her for which she was grateful. The last thing she wanted was for Johnny to pick up on the tension between them.

Once they reached the bedroom, Cesar searched everything above the floor. Sarah leaned over the toy box in case it had been put inside. Johnny explored his closet, then lifted the bottom of the covers to look under the bed.

"I found it!" Johnny called to them.

"Bravo, mon fils."

"Hey—what's this?"

Too late Sarah remembered she'd hidden something there.

The moment Cesar glimpsed the cane, Sarah was afraid there'd be an explosion. Johnny handed it to him.

While Sarah held her breath, Cesar examined it. "This belonged to my brother when he needed help walking. I wonder what it's doing under *your* bed?"

Johnny hunched his shoulders in true Falcon fashion. "Maybe Marie-Claire was playing with it and didn't want her daddy to know."

"Maybe," he said in a voice that sounded far away. Fearing the worst Sarah said, "Johnny? Will you please take Albert to Marie-Claire?"

"Okay. Do you want me to give Uncle Luc back his cane?"

"No," came the definitive response.

"Cos you don't want him to get mad, right?"

When his father didn't answer, he ran out of the room.

Nervous, Sarah turned to Cesar. "Olivia gave it to me," she admitted.

"I thought as much," he said in a gravelly voice.

"I-I realize that seeing it brings back memories of the time you and Luc were estranged. The thing is, Olivia thought it might bring you luck since you and Luc resolved your misunderstanding, and he was able to throw it away. Oh, Cesar, I'm so sorry." A sob rose in her throat. "I never meant for you to see it. Please forgive me. Where you're concerned, all I've ever done to you is the wrong thing."

His head reared. When she looked into his eyes they were a fiery silver. She'd forgotten they could look like that.

"The wrong thing? That's not strictly true. After six years, you could have continued to stay away and I would never have known. It took an extraordinary woman to brave me in that hospital room.

"It's even more amazing that you married me so I could have my son under optimum circumstances. You've had to make all the adjustments without any thought to your own needs. I'm not unaware that by marrying me, you've had to say goodbye to other men."

Oh, Cesar… Don't you know I said goodbye to them at the age of seventeen?

"Johnny's my life. He wants to be with you. His happiness is mine."

"Then we understand each other."

"Yes."

She understood that she'd killed any love he'd ever had for her, but for the love of Johnny he would find a way to make their marriage work. This was as close to an olive branch as she would ever receive from him, and was humbled by it.

"Tell the family I'll be out in a minute."

"I will."

Knowing he needed time, she rushed from the bedroom to join the others. When Cesar finally wheeled himself out to the back where everyone was loading up in the airport limo, there was no sign of the cane.

Olivia eyed Sarah knowing something was wrong. They squeezed hands. "I'll call you when we reach Monaco," she said in an aside.

"Please do," Sarah whispered back. Olivia was

married to a Falcon. No one else could understand quite the same way.

Sarah waved goodbye to Luc and Marie-Claire before moving over to the other side with Johnny.

"We'll be expecting you next month." Cesar's mother kissed her on both cheeks before embracing her grandson one more time.

When Sarah turned away wet eyed, she almost ran into Cesar's father who was shorter than his sons, but every bit as attractive. He gave her a big hug and whispered in her ears. "You've saved my son's life. Bless you, *ma fille.*" He'd called her his daughter. In her wildest dreams she wouldn't have expected it.

"I've always loved him," she confessed so no one else could hear.

"Never stop, no matter what."

She'd just received pleading advice from the man who probably understood his son's emotional makeup better than anyone. Too soon the limo began to back out.

Johnny started crying. Cesar pulled him onto his lap. "We're going to miss everyone, aren't we?"

He nodded before throwing his arms around Cesar's neck. "I'm glad you're not going away."

"I'll never leave you."

Johnny squeezed him tighter. "I love you, Daddy."

"I love you, too, and I have an idea. How would you and your mommy like to take a boat ride on the Tyrrhenian Sea before dark?"

"The *what?*" His tears dried up in a hurry.

"That's the water we look out on from the terrace."

To Sarah's surprise Johnny frowned. "But what if we get too close to the Sirens?"

"Honey—there aren't any Sirens. That's just a story."

Cesar chuckled. "Don't worry. We won't go in that direction. Those islands are privately owned anyway. We'll take our boat to Capri. Since there are too many tourists walking around, we'll just enjoy a ride on the ocean and buy some *gelato* before we come back to the villa."

With Cesar in this mood, an outing to the famous Isle of Capri where he'd once promised to take her sounded heavenly.

"Juliana taught me that means ice cream."

"That's right. The very best there is."

"Um. I love strawberry."

"So do I."

"Hey, Mommy—Daddy likes strawberry, too!"

Sarah loved listening to them talk. "You must be his son."

"I *am!* You're funny, Mommy."

Rich, full laughter broke from Cesar. He sounded happy. After the incident with the cane she hadn't known what to expect. She would take this moment and savor it for the rest of the evening. But before they'd returned home, she noticed a change in Cesar. Johnny was doing all the talking while his father had gone quiet.

When she examined his features, she saw tension lines that hadn't been there earlier. Sarah sensed he was ill, but she didn't know if it was physical or emotional.

Maybe more memories of the crash were giving him a headache, one that made his complexion look like paste. Yet he hadn't said a word in case he alarmed Johnny.

The moment they reached the house she nodded to Angelo, signaling for him to take care of Cesar. He must have seen what she saw because the older man wheeled him straight down the hall.

Relieved they were back home, she put Johnny to bed without a bath. After his prayers she said, "I know you want to say good-night to daddy, but he's so tired he's already gone to bed and we shouldn't disturb him."

"Okay."

She tucked some toys in his covers and kissed his forehead.

"I can't wait till tomorrow. Daddy's going to help me build my Lego pirate ship."

"That sounds exciting." Every day with his father was a new adventure.

"Good night, Mommy."

"Good night, honey."

Anxious over Cesar, she hurried from the room into the master bedroom. Angelo had already put him to bed, hopefully with some pain medication. He lay on his back asleep. Moving closer to him, she saw how his hands clutched the sheet, as if he were in extreme pain.

As quietly as she could, she changed into her nightgown, then got in next to him. After twenty minutes his breathing started to sound erratic. She could hear him muttering something unintelligible.

Her only thought was to give him comfort. Out

of needs she couldn't suppress any longer, she wrapped her arm around chest and buried her face in his neck.

His body was damp with sweat. At first she couldn't make out what he was saying, but it was evident he was in torment.

Suddenly he crushed her against him with superhuman strength. "I'm a dead man!"

"You're not dead, Cesar!" She half-climbed on top of him, taking him by the shoulders. "You're alive, darling. You're alive. Come on. Wake up."

She began kissing his face, every centimeter of his skin and features. "You're all right, Cesar. You're here with me."

As fast as it came, the tension left his hard body. He opened his eyes. "Sarah?" He sounded dazed.

"Yes. You were reliving the crash. I heard you say 'I'm a dead man.' Tell me about it." He needed to talk about it. His doctor said it was vital.

Cesar blinked. "I was told to watch for debris coming around the turn. Rykert had taken a hit. Out of nowhere Prinz's car came flying at me." His powerful body shuddered. She felt it resonate to her insides. "When I was tossed through the air, I knew that was it."

How ghastly.

"But it wasn't the end. All three of you are alive and well. By next season you'll be out on the track again with Johnny cheering you on. *I'll* be cheering you on. I love you, Cesar. You have no idea how much," she cried before covering his mouth with her own.

Like someone coming out of a trance, he slowly began to respond until they were moving and breathing as one flesh. At last this was her Cesar in her arms. She needed his kiss the way she needed air.

While he put one hard-muscled arm around her back, he moved his other hand to the back of her head to keep her in place. Little did he know she wasn't going anywhere. All that she craved was right here with their mouths clinging to each other, tasting and savoring what had been denied them since that rapturous night years ago.

As his lips traveled to her throat, the white-hot heat of desire engulfed her. It had been so long since she'd known the feeling, she was burning with feverish needs.

"I'll help you get into a better position," she whispered into his vibrant black hair, aware he didn't have the same mobility and needed help. Aching for his love, wanting to show him he would always be desirable to her, she reached around to roll him on his side so he was facing her.

"There."

She smiled, wanting to help him get back his old confidence so they could recapture every glorious moment of the night they'd made love over and over again. Still on her knees, she started to lift off her nightgown. But she wasn't allowed to get any closer because his hand caught both of hers in a vise-like grip preventing movement.

A cruel smile broke out on his face. "This is as far as the show goes, *sposa mia*. You make an excellent mother, publicist and nurse, but your other talents need to be saved for a man who can service you."

He might just as well have squeezed every drop of blood from her heart. "Cesar— I only wanted to show you how desirable you are. We can work this out."

"If you mean *your* frustration, I'm afraid that's your problem, not mine. I did warn you."

After releasing her hands, he rearranged his

pillow, then closed his eyes to let her know he wanted sleep and nothing else.

All she'd wanted was to make him realize he was still a man in every sense of the word. If she'd been any other woman, he might have allowed the experiment to continue. But there was no forgiveness for her. To ask for it was wrong.

She shrank from him and buried herself in the covers, realizing she didn't deserve more than his cold tolerance. You couldn't keep the secret of his son from him and expect anything else.

Much as she wanted to run someplace and cry out in pain where no one could hear her, she couldn't. He needed to be turned at two, and again at four. Furthermore tonight he'd had a complete breakthrough with his nightmare. In case he suffered another one before morning, she would be here to help bring him out of it again.

Cesar lay there writhing in physical and emotional turmoil. Sarah's perfume, the taste of her lips had intoxicated him almost to the breaking point. He despised himself for letting her get this close to him tonight. After her betrayal, how could he stand her touch?

It went to show what a fool he really was and always had been where she was concerned. The only good to come of their union was his wonderful Johnny. Surely for his son's sake Cesar could be stronger than her treacherous Siren's call—

He still had the rest of this night to get through, and all the other nights when she awakened to turn him. Never again would he allow himself to be caught off guard like helpless prey in her silken spider's web, one only she knew how to spin with those magic lips and fingers.

A car crash wasn't the only way to paralyze a man. She knew seductive methods as ancient as time itself.

He gritted his teeth. What he had to do was banish tonight's experience to the furthest regions of his mind and pretend it had never happened. When daylight rolled around, he would behave with the same detached civility he'd shown her since the wedding ceremony. Over time it would become a ritual he wouldn't have to think about.

By Monday of the following week, the de Falcon household had settled into a comfortable routine.

Thankfully the bitterness of those first few days seemed to be gone for good. Sarah's tentative pax with her husband appeared to be holding.

There was no repeat of his nightmares for which she was thankful, no discussion of what had gone on when she'd overstepped her bounds to try to show him physical love. It might never have happened, except that she knew otherwise and functioned with shattered pieces of her heart to prove it.

Cesar allowed her to turn him several times a night. Angelo had stopped coming in. Sarah was glad about that. Though the older man was unobtrusive, she craved her privacy with Cesar. Nights were the only time she had strictly alone with him.

In between Cesar's workouts during the day, he spent his time with Johnny in the pool using special arm floaters, or simply playing with him. Since school would be starting the following week, this time was precious to them.

While they were thus occupied, Sarah had time each day to walk to town and get some much needed shopping done. She picked up the wedding pictures and stopped at a jewelers to pick out a ring for Cesar. With the engraving done, she would find the opportune moment to give it to him.

When she returned from town, she discovered both of them on the terrace eating a pasta lunch. Cesar's gaze scrutinized her before she sat down. Maybe he was relieved to see her wearing a different outfit for a change. One of her new purchases was this white skirt and silky orange blouse with the pointed lapels, both Italian designed.

"*Ciao, Mama.*" Sarah blinked. "Daddy and I put the big puzzle of Italy together. Now I know where Positano is. Do you want to see it?"

"Where is it?"

"On the dining room table."

Since everyone enjoyed eating *al fresco*, they hadn't had a meal in there yet, but apparently the table had other uses.

"That sounds interesting. I'll take a look at it after lunch."

"Juliana made us *Scialatielli.*"

His pronunciation sounded perfect to her ears. Their little boy was turning into his father before her very eyes.

She took a bite, then answered back with,

"*Questa pasta è deliziosa!*" The only reason she knew a few words and phrases was because of Cesar. He used to call her "delicious" in Italian when he'd tease her and make love to her with his eyes.

Johnny giggled. "You sound funny, Mommy. Doesn't she Daddy."

"That's because you're not used to hearing your mother speak Italian. She pronounced that *perfectamente*."

With great daring Sarah flashed him a glance. "I had a good teacher." He could make of that what he wanted.

Cesar put down his glass of iced tea. "Speaking of teachers, it's time we talked about your school, Johnny."

Uh-oh. Sarah had wondered when Cesar would broach the subject. Since he'd missed out on so many firsts with Johnny, she was leaving this big step up to him.

Johnny had just finished his milk. It left a moustache. A scared look had crept into his eyes. "When is it?"

"On Monday. You go for a half a day in the afternoons. I've talked to your teacher. You'll like Signora Moretti. She speaks English, so you don't need to feel nervous."

Alligator tears poured down his cheeks. "But I don't want to leave you, Daddy."

That drooping, trembling lower lip got to Sarah every time, so she could just imagine how it was affecting Cesar.

"I didn't like to leave my parents, either, but everyone has to go to school."

"Why?"

"To learn things."

"But you know *everything!* You can teach me."

Sarah suppressed a smile. Even if Cesar was getting frustrated, he had to be thrilled with his son's confidence in him.

"At school you'll make friends."

"I don't want friends. I just want you." By now he'd slipped from the chair to climb on Cesar's lap. Over the shoulder of his son who'd thrown his arms around his neck, Cesar shot her worried glance. He needed some reinforcing about now. It had to be a first.

She wiped her mouth with a napkin. "Johnny? Did you know that's the same time Carson goes to kindergarten? But he isn't as lucky as you because his teacher doesn't speak Italian. You're going to learn twice as much. And do you know what else?"

Sarah had reached him enough that he turned around to look at her with a blotchy face. "What?"

"While you're at school, I'm going to be at my school learning Italian. We'll leave for class together, and come home together where Daddy will be waiting for you after his workout."

The idea had just come to her, but it made perfect sense. She needed to attend formal classes. Cesar expected it. This was something she could do for him and Johnny. For herself!

"Are you scared?"

"Yes. But do you know what? I don't want to be like Mrs. Lopez."

"Who's Mrs. Lopez?" Cesar questioned in a deep voice. His gray eyes were intent and curious as they studied her features.

"She lives in one of the town houses with her daughter," Johnny informed him. "She's from Mexico."

"Mrs. Lopez doesn't speak English, does she Johnny?"

"Nope."

"Guess how long she's been in California?"

"I don't know."

"Twenty years."

He frowned. "Twenty—"

"That's a long time to live in a country and not learn the language. She was probably scared, too. But just imagine if you and I lived with daddy twenty years and we still couldn't speak Italian? Think how much fun we'll have saying *Buon giorno* and *Ciao* to Nana and Papa on the phone. They won't believe it."

"I can say *Ciao* now!" He slid off his father's lap. "I bet Carson doesn't know any Italian." The wheels were spinning.

"Sure he does," Cesar murmured. "He can say pizza and spaghetti, can't he?"

Though Cesar kept a deadpan face, Johnny got the joke. He laughed and patted his father's cheeks. "You're funny, Daddy. Will you take me to my first class?"

"We'll all go," he announced. His eyes thanked Sarah in a private message. One crumb from his table and her insides turned to mush. "Now if you two will excuse me, Angelo's waiting to drive me to the clinic."

"What's wrong?" Johnny cried before Sarah could ask the same question.

"I'm taking the helicopter to Rome for my checkup. I have to keep my appointment with the doctor. It's been over a week since I left the hospital."

"Can't we go with you?"

"I won't be gone that long. He's going to do some tests. That's all. I'll be back before you know it."

"Promise?"

"I wouldn't lie to you."

Johnny stared at him, fighting more tears. "Okay."

Sarah got up from the table and put an arm around his shoulders. "Come on, honey. I want to see that puzzle."

Except that Johnny had other plans in mind. After walking his father out to the car, he returned to the terrace. Sarah stayed with him. Ten minutes later they both watched the helicopter lift above the other side of the mount and wing its way north. After the togetherness they'd all shared, it was agony to see the man they loved disappear into the blue.

Sarah knew Johnny wouldn't be himself until Cesar came back. In fact he probably wouldn't budge from the terrace watching for his return. She left him long enough to get some board games they could play while they waited.

As it turned out, he didn't come by dinnertime. He still hadn't arrived when it was bathtime.

"Do you think Daddy's okay?" he asked as she put him to bed.

"Of course. He would have called otherwise. Doctors always take a long time. Come on. I'll lie down with you."

After his prayer, which was all about bringing his father home safe, Sarah subsided next to him on top of the covers. She'd scarcely closed her eyes when she heard Cesar whisper, "Is he asleep?"

"You're back!" Johnny cried. He'd been awake the whole time. Like lightning he flew out of bed into his father's arms. "You took so long."

"The doctor had an emergency to take care of first."

Sarah didn't believe him, but it didn't matter. He was home now. She slid off the side and went into their bedroom to get ready for bed. Another hour passed before he was back with Angelo who helped him with his nightly routine.

Once they were alone she turned to him. He was lying on his left side away from her, a silent signal he didn't want to talk, but she wouldn't let him get away with it this time.

"Tell me what the doctor said. I can't wait any longer to hear."

"I don't know why." That cold, dismissive tone was back in his voice. Her spirits plunged. She'd almost forgotten. "I told you I have no expectations. To be blunt, I'm exhausted. *Buona notte*, Sarah. "

CHAPTER EIGHT

CESAR needed time to comprehend what he'd learned at the hospital. Two specialists besides his own doctor had run him through tests. After hearing that his bodily functions were returning to normal, and he'd been experiencing a tingling in his feet and legs over the last two days, their opinion was unanimous.

"The bruising wasn't as serious as we'd first supposed. The shock has worn off and the bundle of nerves injured is receiving those brain signals once more. That means you're going to walk again, Cesar. Perhaps not as perfectly as you once did.

"It's way too early to talk about getting back in a race car. Only time and hard work will give you the answer. It all depends on your physical therapy, which you will have to continue for a long time."

The miraculous news made him wonder if his heart could withstand the impact.

He could hardly believe it, yet the tingling sensations were growing stronger. They made him so restless he realized the nerves were coming back to life. Last night he could have sworn he felt Sarah's fingers on his hip after she'd turned him. They'd lingered for a moment, sending a shock wave through his nervous system.

For the time being he didn't want anyone to know except Bibi and Massimo. He'd sworn the doctors to absolute secrecy. Until he could at least get out of the wheelchair on his own power and prove he was a real man again, he preferred everyone remain in the dark, particularly Johnny and Sarah.

It was a good thing she planned to go to school at the same time as their son. Now that he knew the prognosis, there were rigorous new exercises to do. He wanted total privacy while Bibi helped him.

Once Johnny was asleep, he'd wheeled out to the terrace where he could be alone to ring Massimo. It was the middle of the night in the Peten jungle of Guatemala, but he didn't care and knew his cousin wouldn't, either.

After hearing the news, Massimo couldn't talk

for a minute. Like Cesar, he was trying to wrap himself around the incredible news. "Miracles really do happen," he said in a husky voice.

"Incredible, isn't it?" Cesar had trouble swallowing. "I'm keeping it quiet for a while."

"I understand," Massimo said at last. "In your shoes I'd do the same thing. Julie would want immediate results and these things take time. Since you can't give your wife a definite date, I wouldn't want to put her through that, either. What Sarah doesn't know yet can't hurt her."

Thank God Massimo understood. *"Exactamente."*

"In three weeks Julie and I will be flying to Italy with Nicky."

"You're staying with us for the first week!"

"*Capisce.* I'll call you when it gets closer to our departure to make final plans. I'm dying to meet Giovanni de Falcon."

Cesar grinned. "Be prepared to answer a thousand questions. *Archeologo* is now a part of his vocabulary."

Massimo chuckled. *"A presto, Cesario."*

Two weeks later Sarah left the institute where she was taking Italian. Johnny's school was three blocks away. She had to hurry so she wouldn't be late to meet him. Normally they walked home together. The steepness of the vertical town with its unexpected steps and walkways was an endless source of fascination to both of them. But today when she rounded the corner, she noticed Angelo was out in front with the car.

After he had informed her Cesar was inside, she decided not to interfere and got in the passenger seat to wait. If there were anything wrong, Angelo would have told her. A man of few words, she couldn't tell if he liked her or not. Bianca didn't talk much more, but Sarah felt her antipathy.

Between them and Cesar's remote, standoffish behavior since his hospital checkup, she felt like a persona non grata in her own home. Technically it was her home now, but Johnny was the only one who acted as if he'd always lived there. That was because everyone adored Johnny.

His adaptation to his new school was nothing short of amazing. Cesar went over his lessons with him every night. Sarah sat in on them so she could learn, too. Johnny's quick mind had already picked up the days of the week. He could say his own address, phone number and could count to fifty. With the staff always helping him learn new words, he was absorbing Italian like a sponge.

Cesar's pride in him shone in his eyes. Would that he'd look at Sarah like that sometimes. But she'd forfeited the right to everything except to be Johnny's mother. Cesar needed her for that and nothing else.

Lately she could tell he disliked having her turn him in bed. He didn't want her touch any more than he wanted her presence. This was the price she paid for doing the unforgivable to Cesar. She would go on paying for it for the rest of her life. Some days she handled it better than others. Today wasn't one of them.

Unable to sit there any longer with her torturous thoughts, she told Angelo that she'd walk home and meet them there. For once he gave her a look that actually bordered on concern before he nodded.

The heat was pretty intense. She would stop at the shop where she always bought water for her and Johnny. But to her dismay, when she came to it, she discovered it was closed. That's how her day seemed to be going.

Three-quarters of the way up the hill a car pulled alongside while she was walking. “Sarah?” An attractive man with brown hair called to her from the driver’s seat. She looked again. He was one of the Americans in her language class. She’d caught him smiling at her several times. He’d managed to learn her name, but she couldn’t return the compliment.

“Allow me to take you where you need to go.”

She shook her head. “Thank you, but I’ll walk.”

“In the middle of this heat wave?” He smiled again. “Please. My name’s George Flynn. I’ve been transferred here from New York. I don’t bite.”

Sarah believed him. Too bad she was feeling so light-headed. It showed obviously. She guessed she hadn’t drunk enough today and was dehydrated. Perspiration beaded her brows and hairline.

“I only have a few more streets to go.”

“Then let me take you the rest of the way. You look ready to pass out.” He levered himself from the small car and went around the side to open the door for her.

“That’s very kind of you.”

After he’d helped her in and had come around

to take his seat behind the wheel he said, "Tell me where to go." She glimpsed his language books lying on the back seat.

"If you'll drive to the end of this street, then turn left and continue to the top."

"The top?" As he took off, he winked at her. "Where only the titled and famous have their retreats. Is that what you are?"

"No," she answered honestly, "but my husband is."

"Ah! And here I thought my luck was finally going to change."

He was nice. It was her fault he thought she was single. They only used first names in class, and she hadn't been able to bring herself to wear the Alexandria ruby. Cesar could mock her all he wanted, but she knew that stone meant everything to his mother. She doubted anyone in class was wearing a king's ransom in jewels.

"Will I be allowed on the property to deliver you?" he teased.

She chuckled in spite of her discomfort. "The security guard will see me, so you don't need to worry."

"That's a relief."

"You're very nice to do this."

"It's my pleasure."

After giving him one more direction, he turned off the road into the private driveway…right behind Cesar's car. Oh, no—

Her heart beat a swift tattoo. Angelo had already helped him into the wheelchair. Johnny's hands were full of papers from school. He saw her and said something to Cesar whose dark head jerked around in her direction. The sunglasses hid his eyes, but not his disapproval. She saw his hands grasp the sides of the wheelchair as if he'd like to do damage.

"I don't believe it," George muttered before turning to her awestruck. "If it isn't Cesar Villon. When I pick them…"

"It could happen to anyone. Please keep it to yourself."

"Of course."

George needed to leave. Now! Taking advantage of his shock, Sarah jumped out of the car. "I'll think of a way to repay you. See you in class next week. *Grazie, signore.*" She used the words they'd practiced in class today, then shut the door and raced past her son and husband. She dove into the house and headed for the kitchen, surprising Bianca.

By the time everyone had gathered round, she was downing one of the bottles of water she kept stored in the fridge. Nothing had ever tasted so good before. She could feel herself reviving with every swallow.

"Who was that man?" Johnny wanted to know. Her little protector.

She finished the last drop. "A student in my class named George."

"Hey—like George of the Jungle." Laughing, he turned to his father. "I have a video game called Curious George, but it's back in Watsonville."

"I didn't know that." Cesar's features could only be described as grim. He'd removed the sunglasses. His eyes stared pointedly at her ringless finger.

Sarah couldn't handle the tension. "You know what's funny, Johnny? George is from New York. He saw me walking up the hill. Since it was so hot, he offered to give me a lift."

"Why didn't you wait for us?" Cesar demanded in a deceptively quiet voice.

"I didn't know how long you'd be. It's so lovely here I felt like walking."

"In hundred degree heat?" he bit out.

"I—I thought I'd be able to buy water on the way home, but the shop was closed today. By then I was wilting. He was kind enough to stop." She smiled at Johnny. "Let's go to your room. I want to see what you did in school today."

"Signora Moretti said I did a good job!" He skipped along next to her all the way down the hall to their suite of rooms. She assumed Cesar had disappeared to do his workout.

While she showered, Johnny told her all about his day. He kept mentioning one little boy named Guido. It sounded like he might have found a friend. She'd discuss it with Cesar later—that is if he was speaking to her.

She didn't blame him for being upset with her. Cesar spent thousands of dollars a year for much needed security. So what did she do? Let a near stranger drive right to the back of his private property. It was anyone's guess if she could trust George to keep quiet about what he knew. She ought to be shot for her stupidity.

Or go back to Watsonville.

Of course she couldn't do that. There was no place to run from Cesar's acrimony.

Thank goodness for Johnny who chattered throughout dinner. Afterward, she took a lazy swim in the pool while Cesar spent time with him in his room.

When her son eventually came into their bedroom to say good-night, she was in her robe and had turned on a cartoon DVD. Though it was in Italian, Johnny had seen it enough times to know everything that was happening.

He climbed up on the bed and snuggled next to her. Certain words sounded so funny he laughed. Sarah wished she could, but the incident with George had put a pall over the situation with Cesar. He wheeled in to watch the movie with them. When Johnny showed signs of getting sleepy, Cesar told him it was time to go to bed and followed him into the other room.

Sarah quickly removed her robe and got under the covers. A minute later Cesar reappeared with Angelo. She knew what was coming. The second the older man had left them alone, her husband started in.

"Why in the hell did you leave the car?" She could tell he'd been rolled on his side facing her.

You don't want to know the real reason, Cesar.

"I told you earlier. I thought you might be a while and I wanted to walk."

"Did Angelo say something to upset you?" came his surprising question in a low voice.

She blinked. "If you want the truth, Angelo never speaks to me unless he has to."

"He's not disapproving, Sarah, just shy."

"That's not Bianca's problem though, is it?"

A sigh escaped his lips. "She and Angelo couldn't have children because of an injury he received when he was in military service. They've always thought of Luc and me as their boys. Bianca became overprotective of me a few years ago…because of a certain incident."

"You mean the one involving Luc's fiancée."

When she turned to look at him, she saw his fingers torturing the sheet beneath his hand.

"I read about it at the time, Cesar. It made all the tabloids, but it was Olivia who told me what really happened."

After an odd silence he said, "Bianca lost her trust in women when Luc's fiancée entered this house as a friend and ended up intending to sleep with me. It almost cost me my brother."

With an ache in her voice she said, "After what I did to you, it's remarkable Bianca hasn't poisoned me yet. Maybe you don't believe what I told you in the hospital, but when news about the scandal broke, I'd just made reservations to fly to Monaco with Johnny to see you where you train at the track. You can check with the airlines or my credit card company. I'm sure both have a record of it.

"Johnny had just turned three and couldn't understand where his daddy was. I realized it was long past time for you two to meet. Whether you were at the top of your career or not, whether you would ever give him the attention he needed, that no longer mattered to me.

"But after hearing there was a question whether the baby involved was Luc's or yours, I—I thought you and your family didn't need any more on your plate, so I decided to wait until there was more word. But I waited in vain. My pain increased because nothing else was ever released to the press. I didn't know what to think."

Cesar made a strange sound in his throat.

"Thanks to Olivia's intervention, Luc and I got things straightened out. At that point we made certain the story was quashed once and for all," he said in rasping voice.

"I wish I'd known the truth— I wouldn't have let anything stop me from coming. When Johnny and I saw you crash—" A little sob escaped. "Oh, Cesar, you'll never know my agony. If you'd died, it would have been my fault our son never knew his father, or you, your son. I thank God morning and night that you were spared.

"I don't know how you can bear the sight of me. Bianca has every right to despise me."

"Then it will interest you to know she thinks you are the ideal mother."

Wiping her eyes with the sheet she said, "You must have heard her wrong."

"No, Sarah. It's true. The reason Johnny is so remarkable has everything to do with you."

"And you, Cesar," she whispered. "His Falcon genes guaranteed he would be a very special little boy." Taking a deep breath she said, "Speaking of our son, I think he's made a friend at school."

"You mean Guido."

"Yes."

"His mother was there to pick him up. That's why Johnny and I were late coming out to the car. We talked about getting the boys together next Monday after class. I suggested we take Guido home with us first so Johnny will feel comfortable."

"That's perfect. If Juliana doesn't mind, I'll make them Johnny's favorite treat while they're playing."

"Why would she mind? You're the mistress of this house."

"Even after I unintentionally allowed an outsider to see where we live?" her voice throbbed.

"Angelo told me you looked pale when you got in the car. Even if George has been lusting after my wife, I'm glad he came to your rescue before you fainted. Since I'm aware you're terrified of losing the ruby, I'll see you get a modest wedding band to wear in public by tomorrow."

"Thank you."

Maybe this would be the right time for his gift. Or not.

After a slight hesitation she slid out of bed and went over to the dresser. Returning to his side of the bed she said, “I know you’ve never worn rings. I—I had to guess about the size,” her voice faltered.

“You probably won’t wear it, but I wanted you to have it.” She placed it on his bedside table. He made no move to look at it which told her all she needed to know. Why would she have expected anything else?

Devastated by fresh pain she went back to her side of the bed and got in under the covers. Her mind was still on George. She fidgeted for a moment. “Cesar— I think I should withdraw from the institute and find another school.”

His chest rose and fell visibly. “I’ll take care of it so you don’t have to go back.”

“I’d appreciate it.” She was glad she’d brought up the idea of changing schools before he did. It wouldn’t do for Cesar to think she’d encouraged the other man’s attention.

“The Galli Language School isn’t as close to Johnny’s, but it has an excellent reputation. Angelo will enjoy driving both of you to and from the villa. The heat’s too oppressive to walk up the hillside right now. In the fall it will be different.”

“I agree.” Thankful to have that settled she said, “Tell me about Guido.”

"He's the last of three children and seems well behaved. His parents run the Vittori florist shop in Positano. The teacher paired them up for a game on their first day. She told me they've been fascinated by each other ever since. While Johnny's been filling him with envy about surfing, Guido's entranced our son over his father's sport bike. Johnny can't wait to take a ride, too."

Sarah groaned. "Before long he'll want one of his own. It's already beginning."

Cesar eyed her frankly. "If he comes to you one day and tells you he's going to race cars, what will you say?"

She'd been thinking about that since the day she learned she was going to have a boy. Cesar's boy.

"My father wanted to race but never did because he said he wasn't good enough, so he built a track for those who were. Between the two of you I'd be surprised if Johnny turned out to be a dentist."

Cesar let out a laugh that resounded off the walls of their bedroom. When it subsided he said, "In other words y—"

"I would tell him to make us proud."

In the next instant she felt his hand grasp hers. She'd never expected to feel his touch again for any reason. "You really meant that, didn't you?"

"Yes. In this life we have to do what makes us happy, or what we *think* makes us happy."

Before letting her go, he squeezed her fingers so hard she realized he couldn't possibly know his own strength.

Anxious to try out what she'd learned in class already she whispered, *"Buona notte, sposo mio. Sogni belli."*

She really did hope he had sweet dreams. After the way he'd cried out in the night a few weeks ago, she never wanted him to relive the crash again. It had been too horrifying. Without thinking of the consequences, she'd covered him with her body to try to take away his terror.

Then her desire had taken over. All it had accomplished was to earn more of Cesar's revulsion. He would never welcome her into his arms again. She didn't have the right to expect it.

Hot tears trickled out of the corners of her eyes.

Sarah knew better than anyone her comfort would always be abhorrent to him.

Bibi's eyes probed his. "I keep telling you, Cesar. If you want to try getting out of that wheelchair, you have to visualize it first!"

"You think I don't know that?" Since his visit to the hospital, his impatience bordered on panic because he wasn't making any progress.

"Physically we know you can do it now, but your mind must tell your legs."

The wall served as the brace for the back of his wheelchair. The parallel bars were directly in front of him, tantalizing him. All he had to do was get up. That's what he'd been telling himself for days now.

As he gripped the arms of the wheelchair, the sweat poured off him. "Is the door locked?"

"*Oui.*"

"I don't want Johnny to come bursting in." Or Sarah. Except that she had never come near the gym while he was working out.

"*Sois tranquille.* Now close your eyes and concentrate. You can do it."

He hadn't been able to yet!

Damn how he would have loved to fly out of the wheelchair two weeks ago and deck George of the Jungle. The white-toothed predator had been stalking the gorgeous American female who by some miracle had landed in his class.

The man must have thought he'd died and gone to heaven. Cesar figured he'd seen Sarah walking home every day with Johnny and had been salivating while he waited for the opportune moment to make his move.

"*Eh bien*— Cesar— *Regarde!*" Bibi cried.

When he opened his eyes and looked down, he was halfway out of the wheelchair. The shock caused him to drop back down.

Bibi threw her arms around his neck and gave him the bear hug of his life. "Whatever diabolical plot you were hatching just then, keep it up, *mon vieux.*"

He was trembling like a man with palsy. "I did it, Bibi."

Cesar had always heard of drowning victims whose whole lives flashed before them on their way down. Right now that's what was happening to him except that instead of drowning, he was flying around the track pulling four g's.

She stood there with her hands on her hips. "There was never any doubt *le grand Cesar Villon* would be back."

His eyes smarted. "Not without you helping me."

"You know what? You're going to be walking by the end of the week. Come on. We've got work to do."

This was Monday. Massimo would be coming on Friday night. That gave him five more days. When his best friend pulled in to the driveway, Cesar intended to get up out of the wheelchair in front of Sarah and Johnny to hug him man to man. He was living for the moment when his wife realized she hadn't married half a man after all.

She was in for a shock!

Somebody on the Falcon race team had sent him a copy of the news clip showing Sarah in the toy store. When he'd watched it in private, her defiant stance in front of the camera on his behalf had stunned him. But he knew that in her heart of hearts, she didn't really believe he'd walk again.

If she *had* believed it, she would have worked out any compromise for them to parent Johnny short of becoming Signora de Falcon. It was his utterly helpless situation that had driven her to lock herself in marriage for the sake of their son's happiness.

The truth was the truth. After the night they'd slept together, she'd lost interest in him.

Before he'd called with the news that he'd purchased her an airline ticket to join him in Positano, her desire for him had died. At the time he hadn't bought her reasons for not being able to accept his invitation. Much more recently he hadn't bought her explanation that she hadn't wanted to ruin his career by telling him about her pregnancy.

He wasn't like his brother who, though he'd been unconscionably cruel to Olivia, had instilled such overpowering emotions in her, she'd walked through fire to win his love.

Cesar might have broken all previous racing records, but he hadn't possessed what it took to inspire that all-consuming kind of love in Sarah. He wasn't capable of producing those feelings in her. He'd inspired nothing *until* the crash. Only then had her guilt taken over, sending her to Cesar's side with their son.

The last thing he wanted was her pity. He would never wear the ring she'd felt compelled to buy him, a supposed visible token of her love and fidelity.

Up until she'd come to Italy, he believed she hadn't been involved with another man. Johnny would have told him. There would have been signs of Mick trying to make contact with her. It hadn't happened. But things were different now. Already she was looking further a field.

You couldn't convince Cesar that she hadn't sent out signals to George on some level the other man had picked up on. She'd covered up by saying she wanted to change schools, but he didn't buy that, either.

Cesar had a hunch that with everything settled where Johnny was concerned, she'd finally given herself permission to start feeding her own desires. With him shouldering part of the responsibility for their son, that freed her to look at other men who appealed to her.

When Cesar could walk in their bedroom and have a conversation that meant she had to look *up* into his eyes, then he'd talk to her about their nonexistent sex life and what they were going to do about it.

In the beginning he'd been obsessed with the

determination to get his revenge on her. Could anything be sweeter than forcing her to marry him so she would be deprived of an outlet for her sexual drive for the rest of her days?

"That's quite a talk you're having with yourself," Bibi said, jerking him from thoughts about his wife and how he wanted her to make her pay for not loving him. "I'm feeling sorry for your competitors already."

His head reared. "Not a word about this to a single soul. *Tu comprends*?"

"Not even your wife?"

He ground his teeth. "Especially not my wife or son."

She flexed her shoulders. "If I were Sarah I w—"

"But you're not—" he cut her off. "I'm paying you well to help me get back on my feet. Nothing else!"

Her eyes narrowed. "For a man who has just found out he's been given a second chance to live a full life in every sense of the word, I find your bitterness *extremement alarmant.* It's my opinion you need a psychiatrist, but as you said, I'm only here for one reason. Let's get to work."

CHAPTER NINE

SARAH was just leaving her classroom when she heard a male voice call to her in the hallway. Fear seized her when she turned around and discovered it was George Flynn. He was walking through the crowd of students toward her. If Cesar found out about this…

When he came up to her she had to say something to him. "Hello, again. What brings you to this school?"

"When you stopped coming to class last week I got worried. Since then I've gone to several other schools in the area looking for you to make certain you're all right."

"I'm fine."

"Obviously. Look— I'm a huge fan of your husband's. If I were he, and you were my wife, I'd be nervous about a stranger approaching you. What I'm trying to say is th—"

"I know what you're trying to say. I should have known better than to walk home in the heat, and I did appreciate the ride." I should have worn the ruby ring to class. It was my fault. "But to make my husband feel more comfortable, I switched schools, that's all."

He nodded. His gaze took in the new wedding band Cesar had left on her pillow before leaving for his morning workout last Saturday. She had a feeling Angelo had picked it out. What woman had ever been given a ring of that significance with such cold calculation?

"I promise you'll never see me again. For what it's worth, I'm sorry for what happened to him."

She felt his sincerity. "Thank you. So am I."

"He was the greatest."

"He *is* the greatest," she corrected him. "One day he'll race again."

His lips pressed together in acknowledgment. "With you behind him, I have no doubts. *Arrivederci*, Signora de Falcon."

Sarah watched him leave the building. After waiting five minutes she decided it was safe to do the same. Once outside she was surprised that Angelo wasn't there waiting for her.

While she stood in front, a Russian student from her class stepped out of the building and approached her. He was an aggressive type. She hadn't liked the way he'd been looking at her since she'd enrolled. "If you need a ride, my car is just around the corner. I'm available just for you."

This time she wasn't taking any chances. "I'm not," she said succinctly. "There's my husband now."

To her relief she saw the sedan headed her way in a stream of heavy traffic. Angelo was a little later than usual. Something must have held him up. She hurried toward the car and got in, hoping the Russian got the point. Otherwise it meant another transfer.

"*Buona sera*, Angelo." She greeted him slightly out of breath. After Cesar had told her Bianca's husband was shy, she'd been trying to practice small conversations with him. They were part of her daily assignment. He went along with it and seemed more friendly of late. It was a beginning.

"Buona sera, Signora. Come va?"

"Va bene. Grazie."

Suddenly she started to laugh because she

couldn't say anything else. He laughed, too. The warmth of it broke the ice a little more.

"Tomorrow I'll have something new to say."

His eyes smiled. *"Bene."*

They drove the rest of the way to Johnny's school in companionable silence.

When she entered his classroom, he ran over and hugged her. "Mommy? I have to ask you something."

She leaned down to hear. He whispered, "Can Guido come home with us? We want you to make us scones again."

Her eyes flicked to his friend. "Is it all right with his mother?"

"Yes. She'll come and get him after her work. You can ask Signora Moretti."

"Okay."

Once everything was cleared, the three of them left the school and climbed into the car. She turned in the seat. "Be sure you strap yourselves in."

"We already did," he said in a tone of voice that reminded her of Cesar. Since starting kindergarten, she was already noticing subtle changes in her son. He wasn't her baby anymore.

The minute they arrived at the villa, the boys ran

to Johnny's room while Sarah headed for the kitchen to make roll dough. Juliana wouldn't start dinner until later, so Sarah had the place to herself.

Within fifteen minutes she called to the boys who dragged the kitchen chairs over to the counter to help her cut the dough into different shapes. They made a mess, but she loved it.

"Cut out some dinosaurs, Mommy."

Sarah fashioned half a dozen very rough facsimiles of stegosauruses before frying them. The boys got all excited to watch them puff up like pillows. After draining them, she put them on a plate and carried it to the table.

"Two milks coming up."

While they were enjoying their treats, Cesar wheeled into the kitchen dressed in his workout clothes. He'd just come from another session with Bibi. Though she could tell he'd been put through it hard, she thought he'd never looked in better shape. Several damp black curls clung to his forehead. Cesar exuded a virility that was breathtaking.

He asked the boys about school and ruffled their hair affectionately. What she'd give to feel those same fingers run through hers.

"Daddy! Mommy's made scones! Tell her to make you one."

"Maybe later when I'm hungry." Without looking at her he wheeled over to the fridge and pulled out a bottle of water. Something was wrong for him not to acknowledge her in front of company. It hurt. Thankfully the children seemed to be unaware.

"Can I show Guido your trophies? He wants to see them. *Per favore, Papa?*" he added at the last second. He sounded like he'd been born here. If that didn't melt his father on the spot, nothing else would.

Cesar drained all the liquid in one go. "Tell you what. After you're through eating and have washed your hands, bring him to the den."

On that note he left the kitchen giving her the impression he couldn't get away from her fast enough. Though torn apart inside, she managed to finish feeding the boys without breaking down. When they declared themselves full, she made certain they visited Johnny's bathroom on the way to the den.

As Sarah was putting the last dish in the cupboard, Juliana appeared. They discussed the menu for dinner. In this heat they decided on a light meal of fish salad and fruit. With that accomplished she went out to the pool where Bianca was watering some plants. Sarah asked her for Luc's phone number.

For once the older woman obliged her without eyeing her as if she'd just crawled out from under a rock. Relieved on that point, she sat down in one of the deck chairs to call Olivia. She needed a friend to talk to. Unfortunately her sister-in-law was out, so Sarah left the message for her to call back when she could.

Needing something to occupy her mind until dinner, she retraced her steps to the kitchen and sat down at the table to do her homework. Within another half hour Guido's mother came to pick up her son.

Considering that neither of them spoke the other's language beyond a beginner's proficiency, they communicated well enough. Luckily his mother had a friendly disposition that put Sarah at ease. They made arrangements for Johnny to go to their house after school on Wednesday when Guido's mother didn't have to work.

Later, through the dinner hour and Johnny's

bedtime that followed, Sarah got the distinct impression Cesar was angry with her about something specific. A problem that was over and above what he could never forgive her for. But she had to wait until Angelo had helped him to bed after his last workout session before she could get to the bottom of it.

As soon as they were alone, she sat up and turned on the light. He was lying on his back. She'd come to think of it as the position he used when he had something to get off his chest. Well, for once she was ready and waiting for him.

"Whatever's wrong, please tell me now and I'll attempt to remedy it if I can," she said without preamble.

He didn't pretend not to understand. "While Angelo was waiting for you today, he saw George pull up in his Fiat and go inside your school."

George again. She might have known.

"When George came back out alone, Angelo followed him to an apartment building before returning to school. That's when he saw another man bothering you."

She sucked in her breath. "I didn't encourage either of them."

"I'm not accusing you, Sarah. You're a beautiful woman. Every man has the right to look. He wouldn't be a man otherwise. However, if George is stalking you, then that's something else again."

If she was so beautiful, why didn't he ever look at her like she was? Except that she knew the answer to that question. Beauty was in the eye of the beholder. All Cesar beheld was a woman who had betrayed him in the worst way a woman could. She should be getting used to their situation by now, but if anything, her guilt seemed more acute than ever.

She shook her head. "George caught up to me inside to apologize for causing me to change schools."

"How did he know where to find you?" Cesar used a conversational tone with her, but it covered emotions boiling below the surface.

"I don't know. He said that when I didn't show up for class anymore, he decided to look at several other schools in the hope of finding me again to make certain I was all right."

"He certainly did that."

"The point is, he wanted to apologize. He

didn't know I was married. The second he saw you, he recognized you and told me he's one of your biggest fans. I could tell he felt terrible when he realized what you must have thought.

"H-he told me I'd never see again. I believed him. That's all there was to it. The other man Angelo saw was some obnoxious foreign student. He's in my class and couldn't have helped but see my wedding band, but that didn't stop him.

"When he asked if he could take me somewhere, I told him my husband had come for me, and I hurried to the car. If he bothers me again, I'll report him. But if you'd rather I never went out and were tutored at home, tell me now."

He swore softly. "Angelo and I talked about it. I'm going to triple the security on you and Johnny. You'll hardly know they're around, but it's necessary. I'm afraid you'll always be a target, but after your appearance on television, it has increased the risk to you. I'm not willing to take any chances with your lives."

Sarah took back some of the negative thoughts she'd been having.

"I think it's a good idea as long as you triple the security on yourself, too. While the boys were playing in the bedroom, I guess Guido said something to Johnny about famous people getting shot."

Another curse escaped his lips.

"After Guido went home, Johnny broke down to me in the bathtub. He loves his daddy and doesn't want anything to happen to you. Maybe you should tell him about the security men. I know it will make him feel better."

"After my workout in the morning, I'll have a talk with him."

She bowed her head. "I'm sorry about the George situation."

"I'm not," he fired back. "Because of him we've added precautions that are going to make everyone sleep easier at night. In case you haven't noticed, Angelo has become attached to you and Johnny. You couldn't ask for a better watchdog."

"He's been helping me with my Italian."

"That's what he told me. He said you have a good ear. That's high praise coming from him."

Much as Sarah loved hearing that, she craved approbation from the one man who couldn't give it to her.

"I like him a lot." His devotion to Cesar made her a fan for life.

Needing the darkness to hide her tears, she turned off the light and lay back down on her side away from him.

"I've heard from Massimo."

Surprised he still wanted to talk, she turned her head toward him. "Are they already in Italy?"

"No. They'll be arriving in Positano on Friday and will stay with us for a week before going on to Bellagio."

"I bet you can't wait to see him. The two musketeers together after such a long time."

"Make that four. Johnny and Nicky have joined us."

All the satisfaction of a proud father was contained in his deep voice. It spoke volumes. Once again guilt stabbed her for depriving him of the joy of his son before the crash.

"Have you met Julie?"

"No. We've only talked on the phone. I'd planned to attend their wedding in Milan, but they called it off. Later on Massimo rang me from Guatemala to tell let me know the ceremony had taken place there."

Sarah could hear a story behind that, but she knew Cesar would never share it with her.

"They e-mailed me some pictures. You and Johnny can look at them on the computer in the den."

"We'll do it tomorrow. Which one of them does their baby resemble the most?"

"Oddly enough both of them, even though they're not the biological parents."

"What?"

"Nicky's the son of her brother, and Massimo's sister. They were killed in a car accident. In the will they drew up before he was born, my cousin was named the legal guardian in the case of their deaths. No one could have foreseen that day coming, least of all Massimo.

"He flew to California before the funeral. I wanted to attend, but it was on the eve of a race. With my sponsor depending on me, I couldn't pull out. So I missed being there for him.

"It seems that's where he and Julie met for the first time. To my shock, and that of my bachelor cousin, he fell deeply in love. While he was in Sonoma, one thing led to another and she ended up flying to Bellagio with him to help take care of Nicky. Now they're a family and have adopted him legally."

"How amazing and marvelous for the three of them. Is there anything special you'd like to plan while they're here?"

"After coming from the jungle, they'll probably want to laze around the pool for the first few days and relax."

"That makes sense with a baby." It would also be easier on Cesar who had to stay on top of his therapy. "Johnny can't wait to ask him if he's seen any boas. He learned about them in class the other day."

"I have no doubt Massimo will be able to tell him some tales guaranteed to give him nightmares. I'll have to screen them first."

"That's the problem with Johnny. He loves to talk about all the scary things, but then he scares himself to death."

"Sounds like someone else I know," he drawled.

Sarah gasped quietly. For just a moment Cesar had become the charming tease she'd fallen madly in love with at seventeen. She couldn't believe it.

"If you're referring to my fear of sharks, I wouldn't have developed a phobia if you hadn't pretended one was circling us."

"I really had you going there for a while and couldn't resist. It served you right for watching *Jaws* too many times."

She'd clung to him out of fear until he'd started roaring with laughter. By then it was too late to be mad at him because he'd begun kissing her with a passion she could never have imagined. With the sun shining down on them in the middle of the swells, the taste of his mouth and the salt spray had ignited her inside and out.

Sarah had thought she'd die from the thrill of being in the arms of Cesar Villon, the racing sensation who'd become the world's greatest heartthrob. Back then he'd been bigger than life to her.

He was much bigger to her now in an entirely new way. Not only had Cesar proven to be a superb father, but he was also a man who, like the mythical phoenix, had risen from the ashes. He reminded her of that great bird who was said to regenerate when hurt or wounded by a foe, thus being almost immortal.

Fate had wounded her husband, yet his work

ethic in the face of soul-destroying odds was the stuff that gave rise to legends.

"Has our son seen it?"

His low voice stirred her out of her thoughts. "Seen what?"

"Jaws."

"No," she whispered. "Not yet."

"I'll go through my CD collection tomorrow and Johnny-proof it. After the way Guido and Johnny went through all the stuff in my den, I've a feeling nothing's going to be safe around this house."

"I think you're right," she murmured, but her mind wasn't on Guido. She'd just experienced an adrenaline rush because that meant Cesar possessed a copy of the *Jaws* movie. But the sensation quickly subsided when she realized that if he ever watched it and remembered their time in the sea, the memories hadn't driven him to get in touch with her.

She wouldn't be lying in this bed if she hadn't come to him with a gift he couldn't refuse.

Cesar's feelings for her were as dead as the driftwood that washed up on the beach at Carmel. You could do a lot of things with driftwood for decoration, but you could never make it go back to be a living tree.

She was thankful he couldn't read her mind, or he'd use the analogy to mock his present physical condition. He didn't believe he would ever walk again, but being the hero he was, he would give it his best shot anyway.

Having a son who idolized him had inculcated Cesar with the desire to be the right role model no matter what.

Sarah loved him with a ferocity that continued to grow in quantum leaps. As she buried her face in the pillow, she heard a noise on the other side of the room.

"Mommy? Daddy?"

"What is it, *piccolo*?"

"There's something in my room."

Cesar patted the space between him and Sarah. "Come up here."

Johnny needed no urging from his father to climb onto the bed and get under the covers. This was a first for him. "It made a scary sound."

She kissed his forehead. "I'll go check."

Sure enough when she crossed the floor to his room, she heard a buzzing in the window. Afraid of sharks, not bees, she gave it a swat with one of Johnny's school papers. On her return to the master bedroom, she turned on the overhead light.

"You were right. Here's our culprit."

"Is it dead?"

"This bee is deader than a doornail."

"A doornail's not dead, Mommy."

Cesar laughed.

"I know, but that's what people say because a doornail never moves."

Johnny sat straight up. "Let me see." Taking great care, she showed him the proof lying on top of the paper without getting too close. He clung to Cesar. "I thought it was a fly."

"I'll put it down the toilet."

When she came back she discovered Johnny deep in conversation with Cesar. "I want hair on my chest like you when I grow up."

His father had a spectacular chest Sarah would do well not to look at or think about. She turned off the light and got back in bed.

"Don't worry. All the Falcon men have it."

"Papa Priestley hardly has any."

She tried not to laugh. Out of the corner of her eye she could tell Cesar was struggling, too.

"Mommy doesn't have hair on her chest. How come?"

The blood poured into her cheeks making them so hot she feared they were glowing.

"Hair makes men look tough. God created women to look beautiful."

Cesar—

"Mommy's beautiful, isn't she Daddy?"

"In Italian we say she's very *squisita*."

Johnny tried the word out on his tongue. Perfect pronunciation.

Sarah could hear Cesar's mind working. Your mother is *squisita* and deadlier than the Sirens.

She leaned closer to him. "Come on, honey. It's late. Let's get you back to bed. We've got another fun day ahead of us tomorrow."

"Okay." He gave his father a kiss before following her to his room. When he was under the covers he said, "Do you think there are any more bees?"

"No, but if there are, come and get me."

"I love you, Mommy." He pressed a big one against her lips.

"I love you, too, darling."

"Are you going to have a *bambino*?"

Startled by his line of questions for the second time in one night she said, "I don't think so. What is it?"

"You *know* what it is."

"I do?" she teased.

"It's a baby. You're funny, Mommy."

She gave him another kiss. "Why do you ask?"

"Guido said his mommy's having one."

That Guido.

"How exciting. Good night, honey."

Once she was back in bed Cesar wanted chapter and verse of the conversation in Johnny's bedroom. When she told him he said, "In some ways Guido's too precocious for his own good."

"I agree, but he's a darling boy."

"Darling is as darling does," Cesar growled without any bite to it. She loved it when he was like this. Let it last for a little while.

"Johnny's picking up a lot more Italian by playing with him."

"I caught a word or two I didn't like."

She smiled to herself. "I don't suppose you said those words at the same age."

"With Luc and my older cousins around all the time, I probably said a lot more."

"Well, he's our first, so we don't have to worry about him being corrupted quite so fast."

Until the words flew out of her mouth, she didn't realize what she'd just said.

"Y-you know what I meant," she stammered.

"I'm afraid I do." The icy mockery was back. "You *will* insist on your fairy tales. Be very careful they don't become your ruination, Sarah."

By Wednesday Sarah had employed Bianca's help to have a crib for Nicky delivered from town. She'd asked Angelo to set it up in the guest bedroom Luc and Olivia had used. Up until now, Cesar's Positano home had been his bachelor retreat from the world and didn't contain such things.

He couldn't have made it more clear on Monday night that there would never be one of *his* babies in residence, but with all his extended family having children, Sarah felt a crib for them had become a necessity when they came for visits.

She and Johnny had sat at Cesar's computer to view the pictures of Massimo with his wife and their baby. Years earlier he'd shown Sarah wallet-size photos of his cousin. He was dark and handsome like Cesar, but the other two were golden blondes who looked out of place among the natives.

They lived in a real jungle among ancient Mayan ruins. Johnny couldn't wait for them to come. Sarah was excited, too. Yet oddly enough, as the time grew closer Cesar's behavior around her grew more remote than ever. She hated the tension between them.

Since Massimo was his favorite person, she couldn't understand his brooding mood…unless he was dreading the moment when his cousin would first see him bound to a wheelchair. They'd both been so adventurous all their lives, it had to be killing Cesar now.

To heighten her pain, when she and Johnny got home from school on Thursday, they discovered he'd flown to Rome for another checkup at the hospital without warning them in advance. Johnny handled it much better than he'd done the first time. Not so Sarah who grew alarmed when Bibi was nowhere to be found to give her input on his condition or state of mind.

Maybe his appointment had always been scheduled. Sarah just wished he hadn't excluded her from something so important. In truth she wanted to go to his checkups with him. Where was it all going to end? Contrary to his accusations, she wasn't living in a fairy tale.

Sarah had gone into this marriage with her eyes wide-open. She could put up with anything except his unnecessary cruelty to her when it came to his physical health. If he was suffering from headaches or more flashbacks of the crash, she would be the last person to know about it. Where he was concerned, the only way she found out anything was by accident.

When he came to bed that night, he refused to discuss his visit to the doctor with her. Lying on his side turned away from her, no one could shut her down faster than Cesar delivering one of his wintry rebukes. With the assertion that all he wanted to do was go to sleep, he might as well be living on a distant planet.

Angelo brought her and Johnny home from school on Friday. To his disappointment their company still hadn't arrived. After the sleepless night she'd been forced to live through suffering in silence, she experienced some apprehension about the weekend ahead of them.

Normally Cesar was there to greet Johnny and

take a swim with him in the pool. Not today. According to Bianca, Cesar was still in the gym. Sarah thought of it as his man-cave, a place where he could go to be totally alone. She didn't dare bother him there. Only Bibi had that privilege, and even she was off-limits when she wasn't actually running him through his exercises.

Her heart ached for him. For him to behave like this, she began to think he'd been dreading Massimo's visit all along. It wasn't any different from the way he'd shut out his family at the hospital. Not even his brother had been welcome.

Cesar's pain was all tied up with his pride. She wished she could help him, but how? Johnny had definitely been the catalyst to make him get out of that hospital bed and start living again. But what kind of living was this if he couldn't enjoy his best friend?

Luc had called several times wanting to see him again on a quickie visit, but Cesar had come up with excuses to prevent it. Friends and colleagues from his racing team deluged him with phone calls and e-mails. Except for taking his parents' phone calls, he wasn't having any of it.

Johnny was the only one he allowed inside his

heart. Cesar was fast becoming a recluse, even from Sarah who shared his bed every night. She couldn't bear it. The pretense that everything was fine would be hard to keep up in front of Massimo who would see right through it.

She was almost tempted to tell him not to come yet, but she couldn't do that. Cesar wouldn't forgive her for interfering in what he would consider none of her damn business.

Together she and Johnny got ready for their guests. He put on his favorite T-rex shirt and shorts, and his new shoes that Cesar had bought him. They flashed red lights when he walked. Sarah chose to wear one of her new purchases. It was a kelly-green silk blouse and tan pleated pants, another Italian designer outfit that made her feel casual yet elegant.

Wanting to look especially good for Cesar's closest friend and his new wife, she took time applying her coral lipstick and black eyeliner. Slowly she brushed her hair until it glistened like dark mink in the light. Being in the sun every day had given her skin a golden glow.

After putting on her favorite mango scented lotion, she gathered Johnny from his room where he was playing with his miniature race cars. The metallic black Faucon was already looking rather the worse for wear. Together they went out to the terrace, leaving the suite empty for Cesar when he chose to get ready for their company.

Cesar suddenly wheeled out to the patio. Sarah's breath lodged in her throat.

With his black curly hair a little longer, and his olive skin clean-shaven, he looked fantastic in a new pair of white cargo pants and a tight fitting, navy and white striped cotton sport shirt. The kind with the short sleeves that emphasized his powerful arms. His clothes fit him to perfection, revealing broad shoulders and hard-muscled thighs and legs.

She couldn't help but compare him to the bearded, depressed man she'd walked in on at the hospital weeks ago. Yet she had to admit that both men filled her eyes and heart so there was no room for anyone else.

He was the epitome of the Italian male that women the world over fantasized about. He always smelled so good. Cesar lacked for nothing but the wedding band she'd bought him. The one he still hadn't started to wear and probably never would.

His dark fringed eyes, shot with silver in the late afternoon light, zoomed in on his son. If he'd even glanced at Sarah, it would have been a covert regard. He'd managed to make her feel invisible.

"I just had a call from Massimo. They'll be arriving any minute now. Come with me, *piccolo,* and we'll greet them."

"Hooray!"

Sarah followed them through the rear of the villa to the outside portico. Knowing how bitter-sweet this reunion was going to be, her soul cried out for her husband. She would gladly take on his suffering if she could.

When she caught up to them, Cesar had pulled Johnny onto his lap. Seconds later the airport limo pulled in to the driveway and came to a stop. Sarah watched a tall, dark-haired Massimo emerge from the back first.

"Ciao, Cesario!"

So much deep emotion was conveyed in those two words as he raced to greet her husband.

Sarah's glance flicked to Johnny who had slid off Cesar's lap to stare up at the brilliant archae-ologist his father had told him about.

Then the strangest phenomenon happened.

As if it were the most natural thing in the world, Cesar got up out of the wheelchair and took half a dozen careful steps toward his cousin to embrace him.

Surely she had to be dreaming. This had to be one of those out-of-body experiences, only it had happened to Cesar, not to her.

"Daddy—you can walk!"

CHAPTER TEN

JOHNNY had just said the words Sarah hadn't been able to articulate because her mouth and body felt like they were stuffed with cotton.

Soon Massimo's blond wife, Julie, approached carrying their son. She stared in shock at the two men hugging each other while tears started to stream down her lovely face.

Johnny jumped up and down hugging his father's legs. His shrieks of joy brought Bianca running outside.

The minute she saw Cesar standing there, she, too, cried for joy and broke into a paroxysm of tears. That summoned Angelo who put a hand on his wife's shoulder and wept.

Juliana wasn't far behind him. One look at what was happening and the cook crossed herself before burying her face in her apron, sobbing.

Sarah's prayers for her husband had been

answered in such a quick, drastic fashion, she feared she was dreaming. She seemed to see and experience everything as though she were looking through a frosty pane of glass. Shock had made her slow to react.

In the periphery she noticed Bibi who had unexpectedly emerged from the foliage. But the solemn-faced therapist was looking at Sarah, not Cesar. It was a dead giveaway that she'd been part of Cesar's conspiracy to keep this a secret from Sarah. She had no doubts her husband had sworn the other woman to secrecy.

Cesar's miraculous recovery had to have been ongoing from the day they'd come home from the hospital. Her mind went back over the nights she'd lain at his side, helping him to turn because he couldn't.

How long had he been able to do it by myself?

As late as Monday night when he'd told her he would never have a baby of his own, he'd already known he could walk. That's why he'd gone to Rome again. His doctors and staff had to be overjoyed for him.

But he'd been adamant about keeping *her* out of the loop.

She could still hear the things he'd said to her to quash any hope that he would ever have a normal life.

You will insist on living your fairy tales. Be very careful they're not your ruination.

Those words had been a warning. It was evident he'd been planning this moment for weeks. When he sprang his surprise on everyone, he didn't want her getting any ideas that now he was better, anything was going to change between them.

Standing there with Massimo while he celebrated his return to a full life, she realized this was his revenge for what she'd done to him.

She understood it. She deserved it. She would keep her pain to herself and live with it, but right now she couldn't hold back her joy at his recovery. This was what she'd been praying for since seeing the crash on television.

Sarah ran blindly toward him, uncaring of her tears. She threw her arms around his waist from behind, hugging him hard.

"Thank God, Cesar. Thank God," she whispered against his strong, warm back.

His body stiffened at the contact. She knew she repulsed him, but she was also aware he was probably too unsteady to handle anyone's weight against him just yet.

By now Bibi had pushed the wheelchair over to him so he could hold on to the handles. Naturally his balance would be a little off until he grew stronger.

"Look, Mommy! Daddy can push *me!*" To everyone's amusement, Johnny had climbed into the wheelchair Cesar had recently vacated.

She let go of her husband and leaned over Johnny to hug him. "Can you believe it?" she cried, delirious with happiness. "Your daddy can walk again! Pretty soon you'll be able to go swimming in the ocean together."

He looked over his shoulder at his father. "I knew you'd get better cos mommy said your astronaut suit would protect you."

Everyone laughed at his comment.

"That it did," Cesar said in a thick-toned voice.

Her husband's eyes met Sarah's in recognition of an earlier conversation before he began pushing the wheelchair. He took slow, deliberate steps. Bibi hovered in case he needed help, but Sarah could have told the other woman to leave well enough alone. Cesar was on his feet now. The phoenix had definitely risen and would do the rest of this by himself.

Suddenly aware of their guests, she hurriedly turned to Massimo and his wife who were following everyone into the villa. The three of them hugged.

"Forgive me for ignoring you."

Massimo's eyes were suspiciously bright as they smiled into hers. "We're all in shock."

Sarah nodded before her gaze darted to Julie. His wife's attractive features glistened with tears. She was shaking her head. "Things like this just don't happen."

"I know. I still can't believe it. It's going to take me time to absorb the wonder of it, yet there he is. Walking!"

"It's incredible."

"So's this little boy of yours. He's absolutely adorable. Can I hold him?"

"Of course."

Trembling, Sarah reached for Nicky, needing to feel his warm, compact body in her arms. "We have a crib set up for you."

"Bless you."

They both laughed through their tears.

"I know how hard it is taking a child on a long flight. To think you've come all the way from Central America."

"I must admit we're glad to be here at last."

"Cesar and I don't want you to do anything more than relax around the pool. Johnny and I will help take care of this little guy."

"That sounds heavenly."

"Come on. While our husbands catch up, I'll show you to your room."

When they reached it, Julie turned to her. "Isn't it amazing that our husbands married California girls? I feel like I know you already."

Sarah nodded. "I have the same feeling. Someone from home, someone familiar." She rocked Nicky in her arms. He seemed content as long as he could see his mother. "Carmel and Sonoma aren't that far from each other. To think we grew up so close, yet unaware."

Julie put her handbag on the dresser. "Who would have dreamed we would meet in Positano of all places? Cesar's home is so fabulous I can't take it in."

"I understand Massimo's villa on Lake Como is to die for."

"It is."

"Yet you live in the jungle."

She smiled knowingly at Sarah. "You do what you have to do when you love your husband."

"Isn't that the truth," Sarah said in a sober voice.

Compassion shone from Julie's eyes. "You've been through hell."

"It's been nothing compared to what Cesar has had to live through. I can't comprehend his terror when he woke up and realized he couldn't move from the waist down."

"That *is* a nightmare, but I'm talking about the years you forced yourself to stay away from him while you were raising his son."

A little sob rose in Sarah's throat. "What I did was wrong. I'll go to my grave paying for it."

"You know what?" Julie murmured. "If I'd been in your shoes, I would have done the same thing."

"No you wouldn't."

"I beg to differ." Julie wouldn't let it go. "The first time Massimo talked me into marrying him, I canceled it at the last minute because he was only doing it to legitimize my living with him and Nicky. I knew he wasn't in the market for a wife.

"His childhood had been drastically marred by

the fact that his parents never married. It caused untold grief. As a result, he grew up intending to remain a bachelor. The last thing I wanted was to be his wife unless he loved me beyond anything in existence. Since I knew he didn't, I proposed we live together instead for Nicky's sake.

"When we left for Guatemala, I didn't care what people thought. They didn't know we'd never slept in the same bed. I went with him because I loved him and Nicky. But I wanted Massimo to stay a free agent, able to walk away at any time because that's what I knew *he* wanted.

"You think I don't know how you felt being in love with a race car driver like Cesar? The rolling stone who gathers no moss? With his background and breeding, men like him only come along maybe once in a century.

"According to my husband, Cesar never intended to marry, or if he did, it would be after he walked away from his career. I fully understand your terrible dilemma. If I'd gotten pregnant by a man who belonged to the world and made no bones about it, I would have done exactly what you did.

"What kind of a life would that be for your

son? He'd suffer from only seeing his father once in a while. That's no life for a baby. That would be no life for you knowing you'd trapped him into marriage."

Sarah gazed at her. "You *do* understand."

Julie took a big breath. "You know something? Massimo thinks God had a hand in your decision because He saw how much Cesar would need both of you further down the road. He's convinced your surprise visit to Rome gave Cesar the will to fight back."

She bit her lip. "Well, now that he's done that, he doesn't need me anymore. All he wants is Johnny."

"But he can't have him without you," Julie said. "I understand where you're coming from because I've been there. But remember one thing. Massimo told me Cesar wanted you enough to invite you to Positano. *You're* the one who turned *him* down.

"It may interest you to know Cesar's home has always been off-limits to other women. My husband said you're the only one he ever bought an airplane ticket for. Think on that before you decide everything's hopeless."

"Mommy?" Johnny came bursting in the guest bedroom. "How come you're still in here? Daddy wants all of us to get on our bathing suits."

"Coming, honey."

Sarah handed the baby back to Julie. "Thanks for the talk," she whispered. "It has meant more than you know."

"Anything to help," she whispered back. "Cesar's situation has torn my husband apart. He wants to see him happy again. You deserve the same happiness." She reached out to hug Julie before running to catch up with Johnny.

Quiet reigned throughout the villa. All children were accounted for. Everyone had gone to their rooms except Cesar and Massimo who'd been sitting out on the terrace enjoying a vintage bottle of wine while they talked.

Cesar glanced at his watch. "It's after eleven. Don't let me keep you up any longer. I'm sure Julie's waiting for you. Time for all good husbands to be in bed with their wives."

His cousin slanted him a curious glance. "Let's go."

Massimo got up from the chair, but Cesar remained seated. "I'm going to sit here a while longer."

"You mean *your* wife's not waiting for you?"

Cesar knew what he was asking.

"I'd rather not talk about her."

"You're going to have to sometime."

A shudder rocked his body. "She kept Johnny from me for five years!"

"*Cugino mio*—when she didn't come to Positano, why didn't you go back to California and find out why? If you can ever bring yourself to answer that question, maybe you'll be able to forgive her."

He poured himself another glass of wine.

"Keep that up and you'll have to call for Angelo to put you to bed tonight. I thought those days were over."

His fingers grasped the stem of the glass so tightly, it almost snapped in two. "I didn't ask for a lecture from you."

"Have you forgotten I'm your friend who loves you? *Buona notte.*"

After Massimo melted into the darkness, a too late repentant Cesar pushed the glass away, spilling some of the golden liquid on the table. He used a napkin to mop it up.

Grinding his teeth, he slowly got out of the patio chair and reached for the handles of the wheelchair to help support him on his walk through the villa. By the time he entered the bedroom, exhaustion had taken over.

After a glance at the bed to ascertain Sarah was asleep, he stripped down to his boxers leaving everything on the floor. She'd pulled his covers aside to make it easier for him. He visualized rolling onto the mattress before he actually did it.

Once he felt it give beneath him, his body felt like a dead weight, but it didn't matter. For the first time since the crash he'd gotten to bed on his own power. The sooner he saw the last of that wheelchair, the better. When all of them went out for dinner tomorrow evening, he'd use the cane. Johnny couldn't wait to see him in action with it.

During his conversation with Massimo, he'd hoped to drink enough to dull his senses. The imprint of Sarah's body against his back had lit a fire he couldn't put out on his own. Cesar needed total oblivion of the woman sleeping next to him to get through the night.

He might have achieved his objective if his body didn't have its own built-in alarm clock that wakened him at two for his first turn of the night. Despite his mind willing it otherwise, his body waited to feel Sarah's hands rearranging his hips and legs. Ever since the numbness had worn off weeks ago, the craving for her touch had grown stronger. He lived for the twice nightly ritual.

Cesar held his breath and studied the ceiling while he waited for her watch alarm to go off. When it didn't, he shouldn't have experienced such fierce disappointment. It came in a close second to the pain he'd felt when she'd told him she wouldn't be able to fly to Positano. She hadn't wanted him then. She didn't want him now.

He should be thanking providence he'd just gotten past his first hurdle. At this point he was in training to wean himself from her nightly ministrations.

If he kept this up long enough, his body would learn how to lie near her without listening to every breath and sigh. When she changed positions, it would no longer come alive with the need to take her in his arms.

He waited another ten minutes before shifting

onto his left side. Bibi had helped him practice the maneuver on the exercise table. Turning his body while he lay flat was a difficult ordeal, but not impossible.

As he reached around to grab the side of the bed with his right hand, he felt Sarah's hand on his upper arm. The contact brought on instant weakness that attacked his body so thoroughly, he rolled back in place, helpless at her touch.

His jaw hardened. "I don't need your help anymore."

"I know you don't." She sounded breathless.

He closed his eyes tightly. "Then what is it?"

"Today I wanted to show you how I really felt about your recovery, but I couldn't do it front of everyone. Now that we don't have an audience, I can't wait any longer."

She moved with stunning speed until she was half lying across his chest with her arms partly around his neck. It was like déjà vu.

"I love you, Cesar. I always have, and I always will. I know you've lost any affection you once had for me, but please don't reject me right now. I couldn't take it if you did."

The last part she whispered against his mouth before her lips roved his face and throat.

Engulfed by her scent and the press of her beautiful flesh against his, Cesar could feel himself spiraling out of control. Her mouth covered every inch, moving enticingly closer until it fell on his. She was trying to coax his lips apart.

Thrilling memories of the night they made love swamped him. He'd been the initiator then. She'd followed his lead, giving him the response his body and soul had craved beyond all else. But her feelings for him had been ephemeral.

Now the tables had turned. She was making celebratory love to him in the heat of the moment. Pity had a lot to answer for. Her avowals of love were nothing more than simple window dressing. They were the kind that would sound good to a man who'd believed his days of making physical love to a woman were over for good.

If he hadn't been through this experience with her weeks ago, he would probably buy her act. But he could see past her motives. Tonight she was out to let him discover for himself he was still a man who could perform.

"I'm tempted, Signora de Falcon," he murmured, carefully easing her away from him. "You're a luscious package. I've tasted all of your delights before. But you only offered them for a season, a contingency I never saw coming. I learned my lesson."

Even in the semidarkness he could see her normally colorful complexion had lost color.

"You never said you were in love with me."

The blood pounded at his temples. "After coming back to you year after year until you were old enough for your father to consider giving you to me in marriage, I didn't think I needed to. Without action to back them up, words don't mean that much in my world."

He felt her body shiver. "In my world they would have meant everything. When you invited me to Positano, I didn't know it was in your mind to propose. If I'd had any idea, nothing would have stopped me from flying to you. School was just an excuse to salvage my pride.

"You've seen the scrapbook," she cried. "I started keeping it the day after daddy introduced me to you. As young as seventeen I wanted to be your wife, Cesar. I spent four years plotting and scheming how I was going to get you to propose to me despite your determination to remain a bachelor.

"But without the words to help me, I was terrified I'd end up like all the other women who dreamed of winning your love, and failed.

"When you told me you'd bought me a round-trip ticket, that was like a death sentence. It meant you wanted me with you during your downtime between races, but the second you had to be back at the track, I would have to leave. If I'd come, I would never have left you, and then it would have gotten ugly."

"I wouldn't have let you leave, Sarah. I made it round trip to give you breathing room I had no intention of honoring."

"But I didn't know that." Her lower lip trembled like Johnny's when he worried that he'd done something wrong. Liquid caused her eyes to glisten.

"The reason I didn't tell you about Johnny was that I was convinced you weren't in love with me. It takes two people madly in love to raise a happy child. When you never phoned or came back to Carmel to see me, I had to love you in silence. After Johnny was born, I poured out my love on him. He was all I had of you."

That well of bitterness rose up in his throat once more. "While I had none of him, you had him five long years."

She moved away from him. "We'll never get past that, will we? What are we going to do, Cesar? Now that you're walking again, we can't go on like this."

"I agree. But right now isn't the time to talk about it. Soon we're all going to Monaco for a few days to be with Luc and the family. Nic and Max will be bringing their families, too. Following that, Massimo wants us to stay a week at the villa with them in Bellagio.

"It'll mean that Johnny misses five days of school, but we'll ask Signora Moretti to give us material he can work on while we're away. After our return and we're strictly alone, you and I will deal with our problem."

Without saying anything, Sarah slid off the bed.

"Where are you going?"

"Where I always go when I need comfort." The next thing he knew she'd disappeared into Johnny's room.

* * *

Cesar walked past Luc's secretary and opened the door to his private office in Monaco where his brother was working at the computer with the utmost concentration.

"To be here at eight in the morning, you must have turned into a workaholic. What kind of fantastic robot are you designing now?"

Luc lifted his dark head. At the sight of Cesar standing there, his eyes filmed over. He shook his head. "Look at you."

"Bonjour, mon frère." Cesar moved closer. Within seconds the two of them were hugging again, man to man this time.

"We all heard about the miracle." Luc stepped back to look him up and down. "I'd say you've returned to the world better than ever."

"Hardly," Cesar murmured, "but it's coming."

"Coming?" He punched his shoulder. "There's not so much as a scratch on you. I think you're a fraud."

Cesar smiled. "Recognize this?" He held up the cane he'd been hiding behind his back. "I came to return it. Don't get me wrong. I've been grateful for it, but—"

"But you never want to see it again. I know

exactly how you feel. Once upon a time I threw it away. My wife has a lot to answer for." They both grinned as Luc took it from him. "I didn't think you'd be in Monaco until this afternoon so I hurried in here early to finish something I've been getting ready for you. Have a look."

Cesar did his bidding.

His brother had designed a new prototype of the Faucon. Humbled by his devotion to him, Cesar couldn't talk for a minute. Luc had always been his number one racing fan. It was because of his brother's interest in Formula 1 racing that Cesar had decided to become a driver in the first place.

"I've made a lot of new improvements. The other day I talked to Giles. This car can be ready for testing in January. When Sarah announced to the world that you'd be back to race next year, I thought I'd better get busy."

He propped himself against the desk before studying his elder brother. "She did do that, didn't she."

"With you barely out of the hospital, too. A wife's love is its own miracle."

"You ought to know."

Luc's brows lifted in surprise. "And you don't?"

"Come on, Luc. Olivia was always there for you. Let's not pretend. I don't have what you have and I never will, but it's okay. The crash helped me to understand a lot of things. I'm finally over my jealousy of you."

He frowned. *"Jealousy—"*

Cesar nodded. "You were my hero. You had it all. I wanted to be just like you, but that wasn't possible, so I decided to drive cars in an attempt to make you proud of me."

Luc looked shaken. He put a hand on his arm. "I've always been proud of you."

"I know. That's what makes you the best, and Olivia knew it, too."

"You don't know what the hell you're talking about. After I hurt her so unconscionably, I lived in fear I'd lost her for good. Ask Nic. He'll tell you how bad it was. With an ocean between us, I knew I'd never see her again unless I did something drastic to get her back. I had to do a lot more than get down on my knees."

"But deep down she always loved you. I'm afraid in my case, my marriage to Sarah isn't going to work."

A sound of incredulity escaped Luc's throat.

"Wait just a minute. What am I missing here? Are you trying to tell me she hasn't been there every second for you?

"Who was always there waiting for you when you flew to California? What do you think that scrapbook Sarah made was all about? You're the one who kept her a racing widow for five years. Who else but the woman who loved you beyond all else dared to enter your hospital room after you'd put the fear into everyone including your doctor?

"She didn't have to come, you know. When all the chips were down, *she* was the one who showed up without any encouragement from you in six years.

"Who's been raising your son all this time? After five years I still don't see any stepfather around. If she hadn't always kept you alive in her heart, why in the hell do you think Jean-Cesar was already bonded to you the moment he climbed up onto the chair to watch you shave?

"She didn't have to marry you the same day you made your demand. Sarah agreed because she's always wanted *you*." He thumped Cesar's shoulder again.

"The fact is, she never knew if you always wanted her. It took real love for her to come to Italy still believing you were involved with my ex-fiancée."

Cesar blinked. It appeared Sarah had told Olivia everything.

"Since we're putting every card on the table, there's something you still don't know about Olivia and me."

He stared at Luc in puzzlement.

"I had to resort to kidnapping her to make her listen to me."

"Kidnapping?"

"It's true. With Nic's help we got her back to Spain on false pretenses. When she thought she was getting into a limo at the hotel, it was one of my experimental robot cars. I locked her in it, then made it drive to Nic's villa."

On hearing that, Cesar burst into laughter and couldn't stop. "She must have been terrified."

To his surprise, Luc wasn't laughing. He wasn't even smiling. "Not as terrified as I was, believe me. If she'd turned me down then, I didn't have any more tricks in my bag. From what I can see, you don't need any tricks to win

Sarah's love. She's always been yours for the taking."

That's what Sarah had told him in bed ten nights ago, but he hadn't listened. Since then the wall between them had grown even higher.

A surge of adrenaline coursed through Cesar's body.

"You're so right big brother, and I've been the greatest *cretino* alive. Your confession has just given me an idea. I'm going to need your help."

Luc's eyes ignited with the devilry of former days. "I'm all ears, little brother."

Sarah and Johnny were just finishing breakfast with Cesar's parents when Luc entered the dining room. Cesar had left before anyone was up. She'd assumed he'd gone to see his brother. Since the night she'd discovered he could walk, there'd been next to no communication between them.

"Darling," Luc's mother cried. "Come and join us."

"I'd like to, but Olivia and Julie sent me to whisk Sarah and Johnny away to our house for a little while. Marie-Claire can't wait any longer to play with Johnny. I promise we won't be long. Then we'll all be back."

"That's good. The rest of the family will be arriving anytime now."

"Where's Cesar?" This from his father.

"I don't know. I thought he'd be here with you."

His mother looked pained. "That means he went straight to the track." She turned to her husband. "I can't believe he'd do this today of all days. Surely after his accident…" She couldn't finish the rest and buried her face in her hands.

Sarah's heart went out to her. She'd learned from Massimo how much Cesar's beautiful black-haired mother had suffered over his choice of careers.

Johnny got down from his chair and went over to pat his grandmother's arm. "Don't cry, *Nonna.* Daddy likes to race!"

She laughed through the tears. "I know he does. Just don't *you* get any ideas about being a race car driver. One in the family has been quite enough, my little Giovanni." She gave him a big hug. "Now you need to run along with your uncle, but hurry back."

"We will," he promised. After giving both grandparents a kiss, he joined Sarah and they walked out to Luc's blue sedan. Everyone buckled up before he started the engine.

They'd barely started to drive away when Johnny said, "How come we're not driving up the hill? Daddy says that's where you live."

"You're right, but we're not going to my house right now. Your daddy asked me to drive you to the track, but I didn't want to say anything in front of your grandmother."

Johnny gave Sarah a sheepish look. "*Nonna* gets upset, doesn't she?"

"I'm afraid she'd get really upset if she knew your daddy was going to take you for a ride in one of his race cars," Luc confided.

"Hooray!" Johnny cried. In his excitement he tried to sit forward, but the seat belt held him back. Sarah was excited for him. To ride in his father's race car had been his childhood dream.

Though she'd never been here before, Sarah knew the track where Cesar did his training lay on the outskirts of Monaco City. Luc drove them past the main building where they were let through the gate to the speedway. No one appeared to be out on the track right now. Nothing was quieter than a track minus the whine and scream of the engines.

"I see a race car!" Johnny shouted.

Sure enough, a flashy red one was sitting in a pit stop area surrounded by half a dozen crew members.

"Where's Daddy?"

"I'll take you to him." Luc drove closer and stopped the car.

"There he is!"

Sarah's son saw him before she did. Johnny scrambled out of the back seat and ran toward the Formula 1 car. She hurried after him, followed by Luc who carried his video camera. The pit crew separated for them.

Cesar was already inside the cockpit. The sun shone down on his black curly hair. He wore no helmet today. His hands gripped the steering wheel that had just been locked into place. Something glinted at her. She let out a slight gasp to discover he was wearing the wedding ring she'd given him.

While she was trying to work out what it meant, she saw the white smile her husband flashed Johnny. Quick as a wink Luc picked him up and laid him across Cesar's strong arms.

In a seat built like a jet fighter's, there was no

room for anyone but the driver. Johnny lay there and held on to his father's arm with a combination of joy and nervousness written on his precious face. This was a supremely special moment between father and son.

Her breath caught as Cesar turned on the engine. While he talked to Johnny, he let it idle for a minute. Sarah could feel the vibrations. It drowned out his voice.

Soon she saw Johnny nod his dark head, and then they took off. Carrying such precious cargo, Cesar couldn't be driving more than twenty miles an hour, but to a little five-year-old boy, it had to be the thrill of a lifetime. It was for Sarah whose eyes grew blurry as she watched their progress around the track.

"Quite a sight isn't it," Luc murmured while he filmed everything.

"Johnny's been waiting for this moment forever."

"I can't tell who's having more fun, my nephew or my brother."

They eventually came around the final curve and pulled in to the pit stop.

"Mommy!" Johnny cried to her. "It was awesome!"

One of the crew who was all smiles reached for him and set him on the ground so Sarah could hug him.

"Your uncle got pictures of you. We'll go home later and look at them with the whole family."

"What if *Nonna* sees them?"

"Don't worry. She'll love these."

As she stood up to look at Cesar and thank him, the same pit crewman suddenly picked her up. Her cries of protest went ignored as he laid her across Cesar's arms like a bride being carried over the threshold.

The position itself was awkward enough. Unfortunately she'd put on a blouse and skirt this morning, which now meant she was revealing an embarrassing length of bare leg to the men's view. If only they knew how precarious things were between her and Cesar, they wouldn't have done this.

"Whoa, Mommy—"

How humiliating.

Sarah was caught with no place to go. She had nowhere to look but up. No eyes to look into but his. Beneath jet-black brows, they gleamed like newly minted silver. His eyes only went that particular color when he was at the height of excitement.

Her arm had to snake around the back of his head to give her some support. "Please tell one of your crew to lift me off you, Cesar!"

He started the engine.

"Luc—help!"

Before she could inhale again, they began moving. He was taking it carefully, like he'd done with Johnny.

"No one else can hear you, *bellissima.* It's just you and me taking a final victory lap around the track."

She swallowed hard. "What do you mean final?"

Halfway around he slowed to a stop so he could give her his full concentration. "This is the last time I'll ever drive a Formula car again. I thought we'd enjoy it together."

Sarah couldn't comprehend what he was saying. "But you can walk now. That means you can drive again. You only have two more world championships to win. You're almost there."

"Five is more than enough for any man. I'm a father now, and a husband who's madly in love with my *squista* wife."

She couldn't take it in. "D-don't say that if you don't mean it, Cesar."

"It's what I should have told you on the phone when I invited you to Positano. When you told me you couldn't come, I should have jumped on the next plane to California to get the truth out of you. But I was younger then, full of self-doubts.

"The man you're looking at has finally grown up. Having been given a second chance at living, I have no intention of wasting any more time. What matters is our being together day and night, and all the hours in between. When I told you our marriage wasn't working, that was because of me, not you. It's confession time, Sarah.

"I'm afraid you fell in love with a man who didn't have enough self-confidence to believe a woman like you could love me. I always lived in Luc's shadow, wishing I could be like him. I didn't have enough faith in myself.

"I don't blame you for not telling me about Johnny. With hindsight I can understand why you felt you were making the right decision for him. Back then I rarely had time for you in my life. Why would you think I'd make any more time for Johnny?"

She was trembling. "I know *now* that you would have," she cried.

"We both know things now we didn't know before. Every time I've castigated you for what you did to us, I realize I've really been blaming myself for my tunnel vision. Will you forgive me? I want to put the past behind us where it belongs."

His pleading came from a soul laid naked before her. She was humbled by it.

"Oh, darling—"

She felt his eyes burning with love for her. "That's what you called me the night Johnny was conceived. I want to hear you call me that again and again, and never stop."

Sarah groaned with longings still unassuaged. "How come you've chosen this moment to say these things to me when we're both trapped and can't do anything about it?"

A smile broke the lines of his compelling mouth. "Are you saying you want to do something about it?"

"Cesar de Falcon— I've tried to make love to you twice since we flew home from Rome!"

"Don't I know it? If it were humanly possible, I'd be more than happy to accommodate both of us right here, right now. How about we go back to Luc's and take a little nap before we have to go over to *les parents?*"

"Yes, please—hurry!"

Deep laughter rumbled out of him as he revved the engine, then they were moving.

"Did I tell you Massimo's going to let us enjoy a mini-honeymoon on his cabin cruiser? They'll tend Johnny for a couple of days while we're gone."

"I've always wanted to see Lake Como."

"I'm afraid you won't see most of it this trip. The bedroom's below deck. But if you're a good girl, I might let you up long enough to peak out of the porthole once a day."

"Sounds like you've got plans."

His expression sobered. "I had plans six years ago. They've been percolating ever since. I'm in love with you. I need you, *sposa mia*."

"I need you, too, Cesar, but can we talk about it when we're in a more comfortable position?"

He chuckled. "The Formula 1 wasn't designed for lovers."

"No." She groaned once more. "It's for men who want to fly free."

"Not *this* man. Never again."

"Darling?" she murmured.

Cesar crushed his wife more fiercely against him. After making passionate love to her until he'd lost count, he wanted to keep her safely locked in his arms where nothing would disturb them.

"I can't hear any noise. I think everyone left for your parents hours ago. Look—the sun's at a totally different angle in the sky."

He buried his face in her fragrant hair. "I'm afraid all I can see is you, *amorata,* looking totally ravished. Did I ever tell you your mouth drives me insane with desire?"

To prove his point, he devoured it again. He loved every part and particle of her. Making love to her was ecstasy such as he'd never known. She held nothing back. "My sweet, wonderful Sarah. Thank God it wasn't too late for us after all."

"I love you, Cesar. I love you—" she cried over and over. "I can't believe you've forgiven me. I'm the luckiest woman on earth."

"We're the two luckiest people alive," he murmured against her throat.

Once again they were swept away by a ritual that became new every time their mouths and bodies entwined.

Finally sated for the moment, she reached for his left hand and pulled the ring off. "Did you know I had this band inscribed?"

The delights were never ending.

He kissed the palm of her hand before lifting it so he could see what was inside.

"King of my heart," he read aloud.

"I had it done in English so you'd remember that while everyone else in California crowned you the King of speed, I'd already given you another title."

He crushed it in his fist before closing his mouth over hers. He couldn't drink long enough or deep enough. When he eventually lifted his head he said, "I should have believed in us, Sarah. What we had was magical from the moment we met."

She raised her hands to his cheeks and pulled his head down to kiss his moist eyes. "It's still magical, my love."

"What a son we made together!" he cried into her scented neck. "I swear when I saw the two of you in my hospital room, my heart nearly failed me."

"Let's promise each other no more heart failures ever again. Well, except for the things Johnny's going to put us through as the years roll by."

"And maybe a Jane."

She laughed. "Where did you come up with that name?"

"In my first English reader. You know. Dick and Jane." His smile turned her heart over.

"You made that up." He chuckled. "For our next child I was thinking something brilliant like Octavia Priestley de Falcon."

"I think we can come up with a better name than that."

"But not now. We've got to get up. You can't ruin your mother's party. She's been living for this day."

"You're right. Just one more kiss."

"No, Cesar. It won't be just one."

She whipped out of bed, but he caught her around the waist and pulled her back on top of him. They clung feverishly to each other. "We can't do this to your family, Cesar."

"I know," he said huskily, "but first I have to do this to you. I've only recently come back to life because of you. Humor me, beloved."